Midlife Fairy Tales & Murder

A Happily-Ever-After Disaster

Corky Reed-Watt *Corky Reed-Watt 2014*

Dedication

This book is dedicated to my Father and Mother (Harry Thomas and Corinne Deline Reed), my sisters (Juanita, Teresa, Annette, Ada, Cindy and Kathy) and my brothers (Robert, Rolland, Raymond, Rusty and Randy).

Thank you to my children, Teresa, Jessica, George, Daina and Leo for grounding me and allowing me to grow and change. We not only survived, but thrived!

Last but not least, thanks to the love of my life, Steve, the husband who puts up with my eccentricities, ambition, and cluttered artist lifestyle.

I love you all with all my heart.

NOTE: All characters are fictional and only reflect real people because we all share the world in similar situations and humiliations.

Table of Contents

Chapter 1: Murder

Dreary morning rain drums on the windows, articulating boredom and fatigue for twelve human resources gathered around an oversized conference table in a frigid room. Mary, Senior Administrative Assistant, seems oblivious to the tension in the room. She persists with her melodic dissertation about a broken copy machine in a voice a quarter- octave higher than anyone would expect from an adult. To the majority of the managers, this is a trite subject that is not fit to be discussed at this strategic planning meeting for *Gerry's Socks & Shoes*.

Mary's low-cut, yellow flowered dress looks out-of-place among the neutral business-casual attired room. A white angora sweater pulled tightly around her accentuates generous cleavage. Wisps of blonde, baby-fine hair and a small pimple on her chin (pinking up otherwise flawless skin) make her seem much younger than her thirty plus years.

Two senior male managers appear to be completely engrossed in what she is saying, so no one dares interrupt the filibuster. Her voice escalates in articulated graduation, expanding the tension in the room like a tight rubber band as she emotionally describes how the copier is no longer covered by warranty and costs the company a fortune in repairs. "It is always jammed and destroys the morale of the ENTIRE STAFF!" she concludes dramatically. Had she been on stage, a standing ovation would have ensued.

Most of the managers in the room would gladly give the copier the death penalty to get on with the meeting; however, the two senior male managers continue the agony with a round of ridiculous questions.

"How much time does it take to un-jam the copier?" (Does anyone really quantify frustration?)

"Have you looked into getting a used machine?" (This IS a used machine.)

Jennifer, the only other administrative assistant in the room, stares at the table with a very flushed face, obviously intimidated by a room full of managers. Occasionally she fingers her thick and straight black hair in a quick motion to get it behind her ears where it refuses to stay. Her complexion is flawless, her face broad with narrow brown eyes telling of her Asian heritage.

Stout and middle-aged, Beverly Scott (Product Manager for men's socks) pulls her laptop closer to her chest to avoid onlookers. She retrieves what she believes is the beginning of a bestselling novel that she has been crafting in the quiet hours of her lonely nights. The opening lines had flowed out like silk, but her attempt to reach a dramatic climax now hangs between the many "truths" she wishes to proclaim to the world and believability. Keeping a nervous outlook for eavesdroppers, she reviews what she wrote the night before:

Wet and cold, soldiers moved like ghosts through misty haze in silence towards a dense blanket of fog disguising their enemy. Looking like science-fiction robots with loosely fitted, dust-colored uniforms and night goggles, most fought to control incessant, physical shaking. Fear marched on in the persons of fathers, mothers, sons and daughters—all soldiers of a truly well-integrated army, united in experiencing the demoralization of war and separation from loved ones as a Team!

Inside the approaching city, men of another race and culture stood with automatic weapons, watching for signs of their opponent. Seconds clicked by like minutes, taking a toll on consciences and magnifying fear until faint shadows appeared through the fog, triggering a series of bulleted orders echoing through the empty streets.

Within minutes, colliding ammunition blasts jolted human figures that fell like marionettes while sounds of fear, anger and despair echoed through the darkened, rain-streaked streets. The majority of participants were too filled with adrenaline to fully embrace the horror, but those who lost their rhythm were killed. The horrible, hungry behemoth of war augmented insatiable hate that grew angrier with each assault. The sight, smell and horror of blood permeating the streets could not be masked by darkness.

When morning reluctantly began evaporating the fog, dark forces of evil appeared stark against the warm streams of brilliant sunlight centering in on the gore. Some of the combatants paused to catch a glimpse of deep blue sky just in time to catch a wisp of sweet perfume wafting in the air from a nearby lilac hedge. Suddenly, a young girl, fresh with puberty, ran out to the battlefield in a white, wisp of a dress. Tears fell down her soft cheeks like gems as she cried out, "Why are you doing this?" The purity of her innocence stopped the battle in mid-motion, leaving the warriors hanging in an abrupt, deafening silence.

* * * * * * *

Beverly's vision for the ending is one that would persuade the entire world that group hugs and closed negotiations between middle-class citizens (with on-site daycare and a nursing mother's room) would bring World Peace much faster than political conciliations.

With such lofty purpose, who would guess that her writing endeavor is an escape from the deep emotional suffering she endures from mid-life, divorce and the incessant bickering of teenagers at home? As a woman with higher-than-average intelligence, Beverly bravely bears the roles of X-wife; mother of three; sister; daughter; voter; Christian; aspiring writer; expert at nothing and achiever of everything necessary to survive. Her personal fairy tale was shattered when her X-husband left home for Pandora's Box. She grieves for the happy ending that she assumed was hers for following the rules, while she bears his last name as a morbid reminder of love betrayed.

Years after her husband bailed, her colleagues had to make U-turns in the hallways to escape her divorce chronicles. By the time she figured out she was losing her audience, she had built up quite a reputation as an angry woman. Enlightened too late, she now laments her fairy-tale-lost alone, but the damage to her career dissipates slowly, like rings of disturbed water around a fallen stone.

The strategic planning meeting takes an abrupt turn when Director Dave's cell phone releases an obnoxious marching tune. He carries his conversation to the hallway and those left in the room turn to chitchat like schoolchildren. When Dave returns, he announces that the room is reserved for the executives in five minutes.

Mary is deep in flirtation with John (Manager of Woman's Shoes), so Dave looks directly at Jennifer and asks if she can research possible replacements for the copier and report her findings in the meeting next week. Dave sets up a new managers' planning meeting for EARLY Wednesday morning and everyone leaves the room towards the restrooms to discharge morning coffee.

Mary waits for Jennifer and they leave together, reigniting the emotion of their copy-machine perils. Beverly keeps her distance, remembering when copy machines, justice and the pursuit of happiness were more important than brown-nosing with managers to dodge the next layoff. Mary, tall and gorgeous with her flirtatious blonde bob, will never be laid off. Mary and Jennifer (as well as two-thirds of the company) are more than ten years Beverly's junior.

Beverly detours to her desk to drop off her laptop before heading off to the restroom. Her entrance into the restroom is accentuated unintentionally when the paper towel dispenser closest to the door automatically feeds out a paper towel as she walks by. Mary and Jennifer (who are now primping in front of the mirror) laugh hysterically, as though they have already shared a joke.

"Nothing works since the remodel," Jennifer giggles. "The electronic water, soap and towel dispensers are all out of synch! It is as though they have a mind of their own!"

As Mary and Jennifer waive furiously at the water faucet in fits of laughter, trying to get the water to run long enough to wash their hands, Beverly cannot help but laugh with them. "They probably will never fix it. The security guards probably have a camera in here somewhere and are having too much fun watching you two!"

Beverly bops on the first stall to use the lavatory. The door opens slightly and then bounces back with that distinct thud a door makes when it hits an occupant. Quickly apologizing, Beverly switches to another stall.

As soon as she sits on the toilet, the automatic flusher lets loose, splashing her delicates. Feeling silly, her giggles escalate to jovial laughter when she hears someone else let out an explicit as their toilet flushes.

Mary and Jennifer leave noisily, but two other women continue giggling about the automation shortcomings as they wave at the electronic eye to wash their hands. Beverly reaches for the toilet paper and her toilet flushes again. "I don't believe this! Every time I move it flushes!" She exclaims from inside the stall. The three women share jovial laughter.

Exiting the stall, Beverly begins waving at the sink to get the water to run. The other two women are now waving to get paper towels to feed. As they leave, Beverly runs her fingers through her freshly cut, mid-length taupe hair, savoring the fun as she watches the paper towel dispenser feed out a fresh paper towel in response to the women walking out the door.

She can't resist giggling out loud as she waves for another paper towel. Why the heck would a dispenser deliver paper towels when you walk by, but make you wave furiously to get them when you are standing right in front of it? Turning to leave, she feels a bit foolish when she realizes that she is not alone.

The first restroom door is still slightly ajar. She squats down far enough to see two black, high-heeled feet oddly relaxing off to one side. Embarrassed, but curious, she pretends to prim in the mirror while she watches for any movement.

Why didn't the woman lock her door? Beverly's intuition tells her that something is just not right. With concern and slight panic, Beverly edges towards the door to peek in inconspicuously and observes the figure of a motionless woman who appears to be leaning in an awkward position.

"Excuse me, are you alright?"

No one answers. Beverly boldly pushes the door open to see the plump face of a pale, dark-haired woman with eyes full open and not an iota of life visible.

Nancy Drew would have checked the pulse, but Beverly cannot run out of the restroom fast enough. As she exits, a paper towel feeds out, accentuating her fear. Feeling faint, she coaches herself that "management material" would not scream like an obnoxious little girl. Her adrenalin is vibrating so fast that time seems to have slowed down.

At the first inhabited cubicle there is a tall and slim, freckled woman with dry and bleached sandy hair that rests messily about her shoulders. She is fairly new to the company, but Beverly knows she is an administrative assistant for the marketing director. "Excuse me. Do you have the number for Security?" Beverly asks, trying to appear calm, though she is now shaking uncontrollably.

"I could probably find it," the woman answers hesitatingly, obviously not making any effort to look on or about her cluttered desk.

Beverly is flustered by her calm. "Would you please call Security?"

"I could . . . I guess . . . but I don't know if I have the number." She is still not looking for it.

"Never mind! Just put a 'DO NOT ENTER' sign on the woman's bathroom and don't let anyone in!" Beverly commands.

"Sure . . . WHATEVER!" The woman retorts resentfully.

As the women shuffles around looking for whatever she is looking for, Beverly quickly heads down the stairs to the security office where two people are standing in line at the desk. With urgency, she slips to the side of the desk to interrupt.

"Sorry, ma'am, but you need to step to the end of the line." This man is definitely not in any hurry.

"I have something urgent to report. Can I speak to you for a minute in private?"

"Uh . . . I can't leave the desk right now." He has an earring in one ear, spiked hair and a nonchalant attitude that defies his security uniform. On his neck she can see the end of a tattoo that is partially hidden by his long- sleeved blue shirt.

"This is an emergency! I must talk to someone immediately." Beverly insists.

"If it's an emergency, ma'am, what is it?"

Beverly hesitates. "Please call in another guard. I need to talk to someone in private."

"Right," the guard responds with an attitude, but he does page for some help and soon an older man with a fat belly and balding head meanders down the hallway. Nothing in his manner suggests urgency.

"What's up, Barry?" he half-yells as he nears the desk.

"This lady wants to talk to you in private."

The guy looks at her with suspicious eyes and then reluctantly beckons her into a back office.

"So, where's the fire, young lady?" he asks as though he is sure there is none. The "young lady" flusters Beverly's feathers, but she ignores the comment.

"There is a dead woman in the upstairs woman's restroom." Beverly responds in a low tone.

"I don't appreciate jokes."

"This is NOT a joke."

"OK. How do you know she is dead?"

"She looks dead. I don't know . . ."

"Well, I guess we'd better go look," the security guard says with a breathy sigh. "Is she dressed?"

Beverly dismisses the question with eyes of disgust.

Going back in to see the corpse was not what Beverly had in mind. Shaking violently now as she heads up the stairs with the guard, her red-blotched face announces that 1) something is wrong and 2) she cannot handle her emotions. To her surprise, there is now a piece of copy paper with "KEEP OUT" written in red felt pen taped on the door.

"She is in the first stall, right behind the door," Beverly murmurs, pausing at the door. Curious co-workers are already peering over their cubicles.

"You will need to enter first to make sure no one else is in there," the security guard informs.

Realizing he is right, Beverly rubber-legs-it gingerly into the restroom. "Is anyone in here?" There is only silence. Beverly peers under the doors, sees the dead woman's feet and purse, and quickly backs out of the room. "It's all clear."

The security guard goes in, beckoning Beverly to follow. Paper towels feed out causing both Beverly and the officer to jump as though they had seen a ghost. The officer edges in to look into the stall and his face flushes. Backing up, he braces himself against the wall and dials his mobile phone, motioning Beverly to join him against the wall. Both are breathing loudly.

"Well, I guess you knew what you were talking about," he says in a hushed tone as he wipes his brow with his sleeve. "Do you know who she is?"

"No, I have never seen her before. Don't you guys check a pulse or something?"

But the security guard has connected on the phone. "We have a dead woman in the restroom. Please call 911. Yes. I don't know. Yes. she's dead. Well, no, but I'm sure she's dead. OK. Yes. I will wait here until someone comes. Thank you."

The officer whispers a subdued explicate, sighs loudly, and then attempts to carry on a quiet, speculative conversation, based on the literally nothing he knows about the woman or her death as he and Beverly shiver together, learning against the bathroom wall. Finally, two new security guards arrive together. Beverly gives one of the guards her employee ID and cubicle number and is relieved when they excuse her from the room. Shaking like a scared rabbit, she slips back to her desk and cannot stop her tears.

For the next twenty minutes, investigators scurry in and out of the restroom while employees keep vigil between their desks and the hallway, trying to figure out what is going on. Some eavesdrop covertly, while others have completely stopped working and blatantly stand in the hallway watching. They all run like excited children to the window when they hear police sirens.

It is not long after the police arrive that Beverly is summoned to the Security Office to give her testimony. For the rest of the day, she is freed to go back to her desk, but her drive to accomplish any work has totally disintegrated. She stares at email, but cannot concentrate. All she can think about is that woman.

The bathroom stays closed all morning as investigators go in and out, whispering dark secrets. Finally, the sheet-covered body is ceremoniously removed from the restroom by two medics in green scrubs. They take the body to the back elevator and out the front door to a waiting ambulance.

Employees buzz with curiosity. The bold curiosity seekers send Beverly emails or instant messages to find out what she knows, but the female investigative officer forbade her to share information. Finally deciding she can take no more, Beverly packs up her things to go, but the phone rings and she is called back to repeat her story to the investigating team. The story she shares seems just as ridiculous as it did the first time: "I opened the door, saw the dead woman and ran to the Security Office."

At 5:45, Beverly is freed to go home. The upstairs hallways at *Gerry's Socks & Shoes* stand empty and silent, presenting a dark, menacing calm. She quickly gathers her laptop and cord into her roller bag, lunch bag, coat, mittens and hat before she finally heads down the stairs and out the door.

Outside, the deep winter sky is clouded and dark, giving an ambiance of deep night. The full-moon has a halo and a small cloud obscuring the bottom third of the sphere. Battered leaves litter sidewalks and wet Seattle streets reflect random streaks of neon colors as commuters drive by in a continuous procession. The air is filled with familiar sights and sounds, but to Beverly it all seems as surreal as the haunting visions of a dead woman. The frenzy of the events of the day reel through her mind like a continuously repeating slide show and all she wants is to get home to hide from her fear . . .

Chapter 2: Mortification

Although her face still burns, tears have subsided when Beverly arrives home, fully expecting to find relief from her gut-wrenching day with her beloved children. As the garage door opens, she catches her first glimpse of a very disgruntled teenage daughter.

Tania stands with her arms crossed defiantly and demands, "Did you forget my band concert, AGAIN?"

Clumsily exiting the car, tripping slightly over a box out on her path, Beverly cannot help but dispute that Tania never told her about a band concert. The ensuing argument is more a protest from Beverly's languishing soul than logical. Tania does not back down and exhibits no compassion for her mother.

After years of excellent schoolwork, Tania now struggles with priorities; boys, gossip, and school work. At fourteen, she shows off abundant cleavage, yet blushes uncontrollably when she is attracted to a boy – usually a wild-looking boy that Beverly does not find attractive at all. Her girlfriends use explicit profanity as though it were true conversation.

Band has always been Tania's favorite subject, but this year she has totally neglected practice and meets Beverly's confrontations with flimsy excuses. Only her undisputable talent keeps her in first chair, where she often gets to play solos.

Beverly quickly barks out last minute orders for dinner and homework to her two boys and then joins Tania in the car. The supervening silence is bruising.

"What's wrong with you, anyway?" Tania asks matter-of-factly, looking at her nails.

"I just had a very bad day at work."

"Did you lose your job?"

"No."

"Are you thinking about Dad again? He's gone, Mom! You've just got to get used to it!"

"This has nothing to do with your dad and I don't want to talk about it right now."

"You don't ever tell me ANTYTHING and you don't know anything about MY LIFE! You think everything you do is so important and that my life is nothing but schoolwork and kid's stuff."

"Tania, I really had a bad day. I don't want to argue. Let's just get you to your concert, OK?" Beverly is in tears.

"Whatever. It's all about you!"

The rest of the ride is silent, except for the 70's songs playing on the radio.

When they arrive at the school, Tania takes off immediately for the band room, but Beverly remains in the car to gather her emotions, her throat aggravated with a dull pain. She allows tears to fall without remorse, but she cannot distinguish if the tears are for the dead woman or herself.

Suddenly, panic grips at her belly. *'Oh, My God! My fingerprints are on the door! What if they think I killed that woman?'*

For the next ten minutes, Beverly osculates between fear, remorse, panic, and sorrow. Finally looking at her watch, she realizes that she must leave the comfort of the dark curtain of night and go find a seat for the concert.

Inside the gym (that smells like dirty socks), she climbs up the long wooden bleachers dodging people, purses, coats and saved seats like a robot with eyes and ears that react to sights and sounds with no understanding. She finally finds a "safe" spot, not too close to anyone, where she tries to make herself comfortable by hunching forward to keep her balance on the backless bench. She puts her car keys in her pocket and unzips her dapper grey, all-weather coat without removing it.

Because of the thickness of her coat, her purse keeps falling off her right shoulder, which is very irritating. She loosens the purse strap to make it longer and hangs it across from her left shoulder to her right side. Unfortunately, this feels even more awkward. Finally, she decides to put the purse strap on her knee with the purse dangling down to the bleacher floor, where she feels it will be secure.

Wouldn't you know it? Her solitude is quickly infringed upon as a gaggle of parents and children fill up the seats in front of her and then on either side, making her feel boxed in. The bright lights and flock of people babbling and laughing around her about unimportant things, make her feel isolated, conspicuous and uncomfortable.

Finally the lights blink three times and slowly people start to quiet and sit down. As the lights slowly dim, a new set of brighter stage lights dramatically reveal the Middle School Beginners' Band.

For Beverly, the anonymity of darkness unleashes more tears and the invasion of thoughts about Tania's blunt words and the flicker of a dead woman in her head. She is not happy to have to suffer through this part of the concert.

On stage, sixth and the seventh graders display the many colored faces of America, from the dark brown of Africans to the light blonde of Swedes, reflecting every color, shape and size imaginable. Some sport baby-faces, while others resemble young adults; some are fat, some thin; some are nervous, some confident, and others very serious. One boy is clowning around with a trumpet on his head to make the girls around him giggle, while the conductor looks on disapprovingly.

On the end of the second row is a wheel-chair with a dark-skinned occupant (a boy) who proudly holds a clarinet. In the very front row are the flutes, all girls, and one is a small and stout blonde girl who has the distinct traits of Downs Syndrome. Many of these kids sport glasses, braces (or both), and each unique personality is framed up with one combination of the many hair colors, textures and styles that endear them to those who love them.

Some of the pre-teen girls sitting in front of Beverly start gossiping and giggling as they pick-up on the irony of a relatively small boy holding up a tuba in the brass section, while a very tall boy with sunken eyes and long black hair is standing at attention, holding a little bell in the percussion section. No parent speaks up against their rude ruckus, but they do stop when a small boy in a full three-piece suit steps up to the stage.

This little boy is the epitome of showmanship. A full four inches shorter than the other students, he has a demeanor that defies his childhood. His voice is as likeable as a smooth salesman's; loud enough to hear; and absolutely full of delightful personality. He even makes a small joke that makes everyone laugh. After his one-man show of introducing the group, music and director, the director taps sharply three times on the music stand. This causes the children to lift their instruments up into playing position and his musical score to fall precariously to the floor.

The conductor quickly recovers, despite giggles from the band and the audience. He picks up the music, sorts it, and then begins counting out loud. With a great swoosh of his baton he ushers in a garish din of dissonant sounds from the students' instruments that loosely resemble a familiar melody with an exaggerated metronome beat. An occasional squeak from a woodwind adds flare.

Three times the ruckus starts and stops. With each long pause, loud clapping and even some whistling ensue. Beverly politely claps along out of habit, not appreciation. She now has a throbbing head-ache to add to her miseries.

Finally, the beginners' band retreats and the advanced band takes their place on the stage with the pomp of pride. Beverly's mother-heart searches instinctively for Tania, who proudly takes her seat as the first oboe near the middle of the second row. There is a gap between the flutes and clarinets in the front row that allows Tania to be in site, center stage.

Concerts allow Beverly one of those precious and rare moments to view her child from afar and admire her classic grace and beauty. She watches as Tania intently keeps her eyes on the director with her stunning brown eyes. Her dark brown hair is straight, cut smartly at chin-length and speaking of the polished maturity she aspires to.

Uniforms for this group consist of white shirts with black bottoms – clothes these teenagers wear with pageantry tonight, but would refuse to wear in any other situation. Some of the boys do wear their shirts untucked and some of the girls clearly have committed a fashion gaffe by choosing short skirts, which are quite stroppy when you have to put an instrument between your legs. Tania's outfit is as perfect as her young figure, with her shirt tucked neatly into long, straight-legged pants, black shoes and socks.

Halfway through the first musical number, Tania's single oboe cuts through the air with pure, inspired energy that fills the room with a low and soothing melody. It is a fairly long solo (for Middle School) and her performance is magnificent. The man on Beverly's left sighs, "Wow."

Beverly feigns deafness, but the compliment lights up the admiration she has for her child. Tania undoubtedly favors her father in looks and stature, but she does share her mother's love of music. Well, Beverly never really excelled at music like Tania does, but she does enjoy singing in the church choir and played the clarinet in high school. In recent years she has tried to learn to play the piano she inherited from her grandmother, but she just does not have the time to master it.

By the middle of the band's fourth song, Beverly's mood has improved. From the corner of her eye, she catches a glimpse of the man beside her. He sports a middle-aged belly, balding head, belted khakis and a tucked-in plaid shirt. To his left is a handsome middle-aged couple holding hands – emphasizing the fact that he is alone.

Covertly, Beverly takes further inventory, only to see him looking at her. Humiliated, she returns her gaze to the band. *'Hardly Prince Charming,'* she muses to herself, curbing her embarrassment, as well as the discomfort of her own solitude.

Powerful, successful people are bred beautiful with long, graceful limbs and extremely high self-esteem. Because Beverly falls short of that description, she has spent years avoiding the stereotype of being "short and cute" by hiding under the guise of an exceptionally serious and industrious work ethic. In spite of her efforts, her baby face, short stature, and impish smile have pretty much kept her out of executive circles. Age has only complicated matters. If it was not for her persistence in pursuing higher education and applying for promotions, she would not be a product manager today. It definitely did not fall in her lap.

When Tania's band ends their last song, Beverly claps robustly and her program (that was balancing on her knee) falls on the floor to her left. As she attempts to inconspicuously reach down to get it, she awkwardly bobs back up and rudely hits the man next to her squarely on the chin with the top of her head. While he grimaces, the embarrassed woman apologizes profusely while the hurt in her throat threatens her composure. It is not difficult to surmise that he was trying to help her by getting the dropped program.

Seeing the pain in his face, Beverly asks weakly, "Are you ok?"

"I'm fine. Honestly, it is not a problem. It was an accident. Don't worry about it." he says through his teeth with a stiff grin on his face.

"Are you sure? I'm really sorry!"

"I know. You said that. It's okay," he says nodding, keeping his mouth tight and rubbing his chin. Then he points at the incoming group of kids saying, "That's my daughter's group – the 'Jazz' band."

Not knowing what else to say or do, Beverly dutifully turns to watch the next group of students take their places with a reddened face and inevitable tears welling up. She is not capable of saying anymore to the man on her left.

As she pretends to take great interest in the concert, she is now absolutely dying to leave. As the concert continues, it seems as if the jazz band will never stop playing, but at least the music distracts attention from the tears that well up in her eyes as she contemplates the day. This band really is good, but Beverly cannot enjoy it and prays this terrible day will end soon.

Finally, the band plays its final song and then, wouldn't you know it? The audience asks for an encore and they play another song. Once they finish their encore, the clapping explodes again and some of the teens in the front rows are shouting "Encore!" again.

Beverly has reached her emotional threshold and longs for the concert to end so that she can get out of this crowd and away from this man whom she is now mortified to be sitting next to. The jazz band instructor takes one more bow with the kids and then motions for them to leave the stage, which they do reluctantly, many waving to the teens in the front row as they march out.

Beverly is relieved the concert has ended. Taking her cue, she swiftly and purposely disappears into the sea of people until she reaches the gym floor and then heads out to the hallway outside the band room to wait for Tania. At last she sees her surrounded by a large group of friends and hurries over to tell her how wonderful her solo was, only to be brushed aside with Tania's own flip comment about how awful she was. The teens around her quickly agree that she played absolutely awful and make fun of her, causing her to grin from ear to ear.

Not in the mood for teenage nonsense, Beverly decides to wait for Tania outside. There she sits in the darkness on a cold, wet cement bench, watching excited moms and dads walk out telling their gleaming children how wonderful they were. Beverly fights tears until she finally sees Tania coming out. Pulling herself together, she smiles at her and they walk side-by-side to the car. "Do you really think it was good, Mom?" Tania asks quietly, no longer influenced by friends.

"Yes, I was so proud! You are very talented and your solo was absolutely brilliant!"

"Can we go somewhere and get some food?"

They go to a fast food restaurant and Beverly pays with a small wad of cash she has been saving in her pocket. It turns out to be almost exactly enough. Tania talks incessantly about the boys she likes and a trifle about school. Her smile lights Beverly's day.

When they finally get home, both of Beverly's sons are sitting in front of the television and their unopened book bags are sitting suspiciously by the front door. From the looks of the place, coke and potato chips were dinner. It is too late to argue about dinner and homework. Instead, Beverly chooses to argue over whether or not they need to brush their teeth before they go to bed.

Finally alone in her own bed, Beverly's mind wanders to the vision of Tania playing her oboe solo. She shares a laugh with herself about the fool she made of herself bumping that guy's chin with her hard head, but the day cannot end without visions of that dead-woman's face staring out from the bathroom stall like a beacon of horror.

With fear closing in around her and shadows waning in the darkness, Beverly hides under her blankets like a scared child with the egregious feel of the devil breathing down her neck. Hardly able to breathe, she cries hysterically into her pillow with emotion and terror holding her hostage. In desperation, she begs God for courage and strength – or at least sleep!

Well into the night the tense agony continues, until finally she begins to feel a distinct calm in the silence; a semblance of inner peace. She comes to terms with herself that she did the best she could on this extremely challenging day.

As the peace calms her fears and regrets for the day, she recognizes it as the presence of God and bravely removes the covers from her face. Slowly, she allows herself to drift off into a deep sleep where, unlike real life, dreams dissipate with the start of each new day.

Chapter 3: The Morning After

On Wednesday morning, Sleeping Beauty stayed in bed fifteen minutes too late with no Prince Charming to awaken her. In panic, Beverly races down the stairs and finds all three kids still sleeping serenely in their beds. After belting out orders for them to get up and get ready for school, she races back to her room to shower and dress for work.

Feeling extremely unready to face the world, she still upholds her own expectations of a mother's due diligence. She runs back and forth between getting ready for work and ensuring the children are progressing towards the goal of catching the school bus before it takes off without them. If she has to drive them to school, she will be late for work for sure.

Unfortunately, on her second check-back all she finds are her two disheveled boys eating cereal nonchalantly on the couch. According to them, Tania ran out the door without eating, because she said she was on a diet. Beverly's yelling campaign continues until both boys have grabbed their school bags and run out to the bus stop, looking dapper with their uncombed hair. She knows they did not brush their teeth and feels guilty the day has started so poorly for all of them.

Taking a quick brush through her hair, she is ready to go, but – where is her purse? Running from room to room, searching on counters and tables, she cannot find it anywhere. She even checks under the bed and in the coat closet.

Then she begins to ask herself the dreaded question: Did she leave it on the bleachers at the middle school? Through her head, she recreates what happened the night before at the concert, which is the last time she can remember having her purse. *'I had my program in one hand and keys in the other. I put the keys in my pocket. I paid for our fast food with cash out of my pocket . . . Shit! I don't remember having my purse at the fast food! I bet it fell off my knee at the concert and I was too distracted to notice after I hit that guy in the chin . . . Shit! Shit! Shit!"*

All the way to work she scans the rear view mirror fretfully, keeping a tense surveillance for cops. Although she has never gotten a ticket in her life, she expects one today, because she is missing her purse. Bad luck always comes in bombardments. The day the family dog died, the kitchen sink clogged (and caused major damage to a corner of the kitchen floor), Tania missed the school bus, and Jason broke his finger. Why would today be different?

The ride to work proves uneventful. As Beverly settles into her desk, she breathes the fresh air of relief, feeling that maybe her luck is not so bad – until she sees the note on her calendar telling her she is more than a half hour late for the 7:30 (early morning!) sales meeting! Immediately she races to the conference room where she gingerly opens the door, slips in and tries to inconspicuously find a chair; but, of course, the only chair available is a long walk to the head of the table at the far end of the room.

The looks she gets from colleagues as she enters the meeting cause her to quickly apologize and explain that her tardiness is because she was behind a three-car wreck on the freeway. Actually, she witnessed it and had to give the police an eye-witness statement and it just took forever. Red-faced with conscience burning, she prays that God understands why this fib was completely necessary.

There is no reminiscing that a woman died yesterday. Sock sales are down and already of list of possible strategies is listed on the white board, despite Beverly's tardiness. By the end of the meeting, she has enough research and action items to last a month; however, the deadline for all tasks is next Tuesday. Back at her desk, Beverly finds her email box full and phone obnoxiously blinking that it holds messages.

As she sifts through the ruins of her desk, Jennifer's low secretive voice catches her off-guard from behind: "Hey, Beverly . . . Guess what!"

"Jennifer, you scared me to death!" Beverly replies tartly.

"Sorry, but I thought you would want to know that it was Bob's wife you found in the bathroom yesterday."

Beverly's stomach turns as the vision of the woman in that awkward position with dark eyes and a dead-white face rewinds through her head. "Bob Schneider's wife?"

"Yes. Mary just told me." Bob is the well-liked Vice President of Sales.

"Really? How awful!" Beverly is truly mortified.

Jennifer seems anxious to continue, "She had come to the office to visit, but Bob was downtown on some sort of business and did not return to the office. The CEO had to identify the woman as his wife." Her intrigue is obvious. "I bet Bob was having an affair and she was checking up on him!"

"What makes you think that?"

"He was always going somewhere at lunch time and everyone knows he's a flirt. He seemed to be working late all the time, too, like he did not want to go home."

"I work late all the time and I WANT to go home," Beverly reminds her. "Anyway, I always felt Bob just liked to tease the girls. It has all seemed very silly and harmless to me through the years. I have definitely never felt he was having an affair."

The phone interrupts, Beverly quickly answers and Jennifer walks away. Before Beverly realizes it, she has worked through lunch. Feeling guilty for not making it a higher priority, Beverly finally takes a break to call the middle school about her missing purse.

"You'll have to come in and inquire at the desk," the school secretary instructs. "We have a lot of lost and found items and you will need to identify yours."

Beverly does not end the call in a friendly manner. *'Sure, add to my schedule'* Beverly muses to herself, *'a traffic jam at the middle school to go stand at the desk for twenty minutes while someone tries to track down my purse! Of course, the alternative is to spend hours calling the companies for all five of my credit cards ("press 1, press 2") and stand in line for hours to get my driver's license replaced . . . And how the heck would I replace my address book that is in there? What an idiot I am! How could I forget my damn purse?'*

Anger has a way of bringing out the worst in everyone and Beverly is no exception. Her anger at both the school secretary and herself suddenly strikes terror in her heart. Would someone have to be evil, mean or insane to commit murder or could someone commit murder just because they were extremely angry or even just frustrated?

Are we all capable of murder? Is evil something around us or inside of us? Tears well up in Beverly's eyes and her throat throbs with a familiar hurt. Quietly, she weeds through email and contemplates her own demeanor.

Chapter 4: Midlife Woes

Beverly's house is petite, but comfortable. The boys share a room, but she and Tania each have their own. She teases that her kitchen only has room for two people standing butt-to-butt and is frustrated with the clutter of appliances on the shelves that do not fit in the cupboards, but overall, this is her house and she loves it.

The family room is actually quite spacious compared to other rooms, but the décor is cluttered, worn and eclectic. In some ways, the collection has not changed much since her X-husband left, other than the pictures she removed to deaden his memory and things she has replaced for the same reason.

Most of Beverly's money since the divorce goes to things the children want or need, which explains the heavily worn out couch where the boys play the latest and greatest video games. But her sentimental collections have built up over the years with a perchance for whimsy, like the handful of ceramic hummingbirds displayed on a high corner shelf or the oddly colored ceramic cows on the table under the flat-screen television.

Her inability to part with things is evidenced in things she has kept, which include a dusty lace-dressed mantle where there are two identical, porcelain roses (twin gifts from her two sons one year), a crystal cross with the "Our Father" engraved on it (from her mother) and two tall blue-glass vases of dated (and dusty) silk flowers in purple, white and pink. Although the house is dusty, it is comfortable and hospitable. Who has time to dust anyway?

Tonight three empty microwave popcorn bags on the living room floor and a half-gone bag of corn chips with an empty cheese dip tin on the kitchen counter make Beverly suspicious that this might not be the night to prepare a proper nutritious meal that includes all the food groups recommended by the Food & Drug Administration; however, her obligation to be a "good" mother sets her up for failure once again.

Within her site, Jason (17 years) and Mark (12 years) are fighting graphic dark forces boisterously on a video game, using the television screen to display complicated and realistic graphics. At the dining room table, Tania is on the land line, elbows on the table and grinning from ear to ear. The nervous twirling of her hair into a tight knot on one side is a sure sign that she is talking to a boy.

Beverly would do anything to persuade her children to work hard at school to ensure their placement in an Ivy League college, but deep down she knows that schoolwork is not a high priority for any of them. Even if one of her children did aspire to go to college, she would not be able to help much financially and there is not even a remote chance that their father, Michael, would assist.

According to Michael, the child support he pays to Beverly covers everything from braces to college. Never mind that he showed up in court with a minimum wage job (after years of making considerably more) and was awarded the minimum legal amount of child support for the state. It is no secret that he now makes much more and has finished college, but a court battle over finances would only result in another kick to Beverly's self-esteem and the court result would probably not reflect the effort. Her pride rides on the fact that she can handle all her financial affairs now without Michael, who is clueless about raising kids or running a household budget that does not include subsidies from his wealthy mistress.

Beverly chews on the memory of Jason coming home from one of his sparse visits with his dad with the bold announcement that Michael had told him that Beverly should buy him a car with "his" share of the child support. This proclamation led to quite an argument about the utility of child support; however, there was no convincing Jason that day that Beverly was not hoarding thousands of dollars of child support for some secret, selfish and sinful pleasure. It is ironic that the person who pays child support (Michael) can count to the penny how much he contributes, but the parent who has custody (Beverly) does not have the evidence to brag about how much "child support" they pay. The lack of accounting for the parent with custody also makes it hard to convince a child that the child support his father pays is only small percentage of everything that must be paid to support a household with three children.

But today Beverly decides to remain optimistic and calls her children to share with her a freshly prepared meal of home-cooked spaghetti (with added vegetables in the sauce) and fragrant garlic bread dripping with garlic butter. Immediately, Tania wines back that she is on the phone; Jason and Mark that they are not done with their game. Be assured that Beverly is not popular at all when she pulls the phone cord and turns off the television.

Tania screams obscenities at the top of her lungs and retreats to her room with an abrupt door slam. She is convinced that her entire life has been ruined by the ending of a phone call. Annoyed that Tania's outburst far upstages their protests, the boys head dutifully to the kitchen and quietly fill their plates to the brim.

Beverly dutifully joins them. The little family pauses for their meal prayer, but only Beverly says the words, and then the boys chow down huge amounts of spaghetti and garlic bread, leaving small mounds of picked out vegetables on their plates.

Anger and hurt have a way of destroying the appetite, but Beverly is determined to give a good example and have this meal with her kids, so she forces herself to eat. She disguises her hurt by posing questions to the boys in an attempt to jump-start conversation. No conversation ensues from the short answers they toss back with their mouths full, but in their eyes she senses some compassion for her attempts. As for quality time with her kids, Beverly understands that she has just blown it for the night.

Flashbacks of her childhood haunt her. She swore that she would have unending patience with her kids, because she absolutely hated the way her mother yelled when she was angry, overpowering family members with heated words to gain control when things got out-of-hand. In retrospect, she remembers mouthing off to her mother and actually causing some of the anger on purpose. Perhaps it was just a child's game to gain control.

Probably Beverly would have been sanctified for her patience with her children, had they not mutated into teenagers and transformed her saintly patience into her worst moments of disgrace as a parent. Her non-aggressive nature ensures failure in situations that require aggression and the kids play on her insecurities.

Her failures are amplified by their rejection of attributes that she feels are important, such as going to church, doing homework or aspiring to go to college. The clincher is that Beverly is not sure what she should have done differently. She can see that anger only breeds anger; but contrary to what would be expected, patience rarely breeds patience – especially when the person you are being patient with is out of control. Because few teenagers are IN CONTROL – anger has often become Beverly's favored response, despite her nature, and she does it very ineffectively.

After the divorce, Beverly's analyst came to the cruel conclusion that the children were acting out because they longed for their father's attention. He suggested to Beverly that she should refrain from being too critical of their behavior during the transition. Dutifully, Beverly tried to be even more patient with her children. By the time she ran out of money for counseling, the children were totally out of control. Although she sometimes grabs for control with harsh words and actions in desperation, thanks to the year of psycho analysis, the guilt afterwards pulls like heavy chains against her conscience.

Motherhood was not always this problematical. In her children's early years, Beverly enjoyed reading bedtime stories and gleefully frolicking on soft fragrant grass in sun-filled parks, listening intently to her children's incessant questions and giggling. Even after most of her friends were building careers, she was content in Neverland; but just as she was feeling the fairy tale would never end, her husband's disenchantment became evident and her world fell apart.

He said he wanted her to go to back to work because there was not enough money (although it seemed like enough to her) and as he pressured her, the children began to misbehave. From then on, whenever they would ask for something the family could not afford, the children would mimic their dad, saying that she should go back to work to make more money. The situation deteriorated and to this day, she is not sure if she returned to her career to escape home or to save her marriage and crumbling finances.

As it came out, she had no power to escape or save her family from what was to come. As she flustered to keep family together and at peace, her ex-husband jumped ship for someone new, leaving her alone to resolve all remaining monsters, hurts and misunderstandings. Life blurred for at least two years as she struggled to survive. Before she could recover, puberty began to release its perplexities as each child in turn mutated and mutinied.

Alone on a financial tightrope, Beverly became very serious about her career, hoping to climb the corporate ladder to – well – make more money, of course. She felt the marketing field would fill the creative void in her life and open doors for career growth.

But true existence sometimes has little sensitivity to dreams. The interviewer for *Gerry's Socks & Shoes* enticed her with rave reviews about the company's creative atmosphere, but the reality is that the Company's core policies and cultural habits squelch most true creativity. Employees who are the most strong willed, better looking, or willing to sacrifice creativity for political power prevail; while those who aspire to creativity and duty waste time in multiple meetings run like political caucuses. The best ideas are often stolen by those gutsy few who flaunt their influence and gloat in the rewards won deceitfully with no remorse. On the other hand, many a great idea is tossed aside as too risky until a competitor picks it up.

Ironically, certain people can sway the Executives nearly all the time, no matter how ridiculous their ideas are. Mary is one of those people and only one glimpse of her cleavage seems to sway even the toughest male executive. Women tend to look the other way to avoid jeopardizing their positions for trite and outmoded moral principles; although there is an under-tow of critical gossip only heard in tight women's circles.

With all her career hopes and dreams, Beverly understands the odds are heaped against her. While she struggles to prove her worthiness, her financial situation deteriorates. The math is easy – there is now one income and a child support check where there used to be two incomes. She finds the creativity that was once her essence being trampled by survival strategies.

Her secret shame is that half the reason she dreams of finding a husband is to share living expenses. The guilt she feels thinking that way has probably been the greatest sabotage to her flimsy attempts at flirtation. She feels she is playing a game that morality forbids her to win.

As a giddy young girl, Beverly fell head-over-heels for a handsome young prince (who actually just hoped to get laid). Feeling brave and heroic she gave away her sweet virginity, knowing that his love was as pure and eternal as the diamond he put on her finger. The flaw in her diamond clarified as the struggles of life stole away her innocence, immersing her into a life of belligerent teenagers, incessant housework, a demanding career and little companionship. As loneliness crept into her bed, someone else shared Michael's and the marriage became what his lawyer described unmercifully as "irretrievable."

"Irretrievable" still seems untrue to Beverly. The relationship was only irretrievable because Michael was too absorbed in his sexual fantasies to try. He no longer seemed to care about any of the things that he told her were most important to him.

She couldn't explain to her children why their father left, because she could make no logical case to make it understandable. In a very short timeline, he went from being madly in love with her and the kids; to drifting away into self-absorption. Instead of discussing his feeling with her or seeking help, he found a new woman who felt sorry for him and pacified him in her bed.

How ironic is it that society accepts one parent deserting (as long as they pay child support); but if both parents abscond, it's a crime? Apparently, the lone parent who stays to care for the children keeps them both out of jail. Well-meaning people say things like, "Well, it takes two to tango," leaving the person left behind feeling that somehow it's their fault that the other has skipped out on their duties.

Beverly's "irretrievable" marriage ended without a marriage counselor or even a satisfying fight. Had she been battered or even the abuser, she would have understood why divorce was necessary. She was left like a tattered leaf hanging on a winter tree with no hope for spring.

Co-workers are good lunch dates, but they quickly return to private lives after they clock out of the office. Neighbors rarely peek out of their doors. Beverly's children have their own friends and avoid her to escape mentions of homework, chores or queries about how they are doing in school. Long hours at work leave Beverly exhausted and her "quality" time with the kids is often sabotaged with arguments. Most of the things she once dreamed of doing seem to be in a different book. Aspiring to be the hero, the adventurer, the loved, she finds herself feeling unloved and the victim in a long, drawn-out tragedy.

In the quiet of the night while most people are sleeping, Beverly is writing a book that she has no idea how to get published. Sometimes, she feels it is her mission; but sometimes she has hidden it away for months, because she has no idea how to finish it. She knows that she cannot finish it until she can find some blatant truth that will change the entire world, but that pinnacle of truth evades her.

Unfortunately, her obsession with war scene on the apex of two worlds traps her in a quandary for the climatic ending. Each time she rewrites the ending, a totally new story erupts, making the ending even more elusive.

Beverly has no experience with war or killing, but the imagined horror ejects such calamity and emotion that she is enticed to examine it thoroughly to uncover the causes and effects on morality, beliefs, and how people become so angry that they no longer desire peace. Perhaps her obsession with war is related to watching the original "reality show" – the Vietnam War – on television at a very impressionable age. She wrote a morbid poem about it in the fifth grade and the teacher called her mother to tell her how concerned she was about a little girl who thought about such things.

To Beverly, war is metaphoric for all of the injustices in the world and tainted life-choices that steal away love, happiness and security without remorse. For her, writing opens up a window to release her feelings without actually facing the truths that she cannot bear. Were it not for her writings, she feels she is nothing but a servant; both at work and home. But in the wee hours of the night she is a talented and creative writer with ideas to express to a world that will regret that it was too distracted to notice her beyond her utility.

Chapter 5: Playing Hooky

The red traffic light seems to dawdle, weighing on Beverly's nerves, while Jason in the passenger seat bops to obnoxious music at headache-inducing volume. High school students confidently jay-walk between cars and occasionally knock on the car windows rudely when they recognize Tania or Jason. Once the light changes, the drivers have to wait for the teens to clear the road before the procession to the drop-off point can proceed, which is very annoying.

Beverly thought she would be appreciated this morning if she let the kids sleep in and drove them all to school. They usually take the bus. When she dropped off Mark, the ride was uneventful, but right now she is deeply regretting her decision as her head throbs from the chaos of the music and banter between her two teens. She reaches over to turn off the radio.

"Why'd you do that?" Jason belts out.

"This drive is stressful enough without the radio blasting," Beverly responds, nervously watching the brake lights in front of her.

"You're always stressed!"

"Yeah! Turn the radio back on!" Tania wines from the back seat.

"You can listen to it when you get home from school. Do you have your lunch money?"

"You always have to have things your way."

"I let you listen to your music, but now I've had enough!"

"Yeah. It's always about you," Jason retorts.

Jason's words hurt like ice shards, leaving Beverly again feeling that she just cannot escape being her children's aggravation. To amplify her guilt, Jason and Tania feast upon their mother's confidence with rude comments and laughter. Silent tears dribble down her cheeks. She needs their love and acceptance almost as much as they hate to admit they need hers.

After letting Jason off at the High School, Beverly goes through a similar routine at the Middle School, but the kids are a little more

35

polite, only crossing with the crossing guards and not knocking on the car as they walk by.

After letting Tania off at the drop-off point, she drives around the block and proceeds to the visitor parking lot, squeezing into a parking space next to a battered gray car with its rear wheel partially in her space. Briskly, she walks the long distance to the school entrance, following what seems likes hundreds of book-bag-clad backs of all colors, shapes and sizes.

Once she is in the door, she has to work her way to the office. Like a fish trying to swim upstream, she fights her way through the crowd of twelve-to-fifteen year olds to the office.

Suddenly, there is a loud blare of an electronic bell and the hallways quickly empty and become quiet. The stragglers form a line at the front desk in the office, some with their mothers. Beverly reluctantly joins them.

The woman at the front desk speaks gruffly with each child in turn, usually quickly scribbling out a pass with orders for what they need to do next, unless they are with their mother, in which case she is a bit more polite. Some of the kids she knows by name and she makes fun of them. They call her Ms. Nelly. She proudly carries about 60 pounds of excess fat under her out-of-date white blouse and black skirt, which makes her presence all the more intimidating. Her yellow-gray hair is long and strait with outdated bangs. Dark, heavy reading glasses hang on her nose at half mast, attached with a black cord around her neck.

After listening to a half-dozen teenagers describe their quandary, Beverly finally revolves to the front of the line to ask if her purse was found. Ms. Nelly reaches down under the counter and heaves a huge, brown cardboard box of purses and miscellaneous items onto the counter. Beverly is relieved to see her purse on top. The contents seem intact, including several pieces of odd change and a rumpled tissue. After verifying the ID with Ms. Nelly, Beverly heads out the door with her purse in hand, realizing that she is already an hour late for work, but feeling quite relieved.

Did you ever look up at a clear blue sky and feel the call of the wind? With the chaos of the "lost purse" ordeal behind her, Beverly finds the morning sun enticing, captivating and calling her name. At once she is convinced that she should not go to work today. Freedom whispers gently on the breeze, "Come and dance!" Her righteousness protests, but emotion and exhaustion have the greater pull and she finds herself driving home to call in "sick".

There was a little girl with a little curl, right in the middle of her forehead. When she was good, she was very good. When she was bad, she felt guilty and where there is guilt, there is nothing more delicious than catching up with things that you feel guilty about, like house cleaning.

Beverly's morning is spent polishing her neglected house with insatiable energy. The box of emotion she has locked up for the past several days unlocks. Soon she is reliving flashes of Bob's wife, dead in the bathroom, blood running down her face. She wonders why it happened, who did it and why she had to be the one to find her.

Her emotions wind around recent encounters with her children, how her ex-husband just stopped loving her one day, dropping her like a dead conversation, as well as his current escapades. Soon she has turned the relief and freedom of what was supposed to be a liberating "sick" day into absolute morbidity. Her bucket of sorrow empties and the solitude gives her consent to cry hysterically: *I wish my ex-husband had died instead of left me! I loved him more than life itself and he put me out with the trash . . .*

Near their twentieth anniversary, Beverly had hinted to Michael that she would like an eternity ring and a romantic vacation. Instead, he had an affair. Thanks to the kids, she has now learned that he has showered his newfound princess with luxuries far beyond Beverly's wildest dreams. It would probably shock Michael's muse, Natalie, that the now-generous Michael never bought Beverly an expensive gift in all their years of marriage. Natalie's view of Beverly is the wicked witch who rapes her of luxuries by demanding child support.

By noon, Beverly has exhausted her despair and tears have given way to the silence of solitude. This emotional release seems to have emptied a place in her soul for peace, which she savors for what seems like a very long time, slouched in a chair, hardly moving at all and nearly asleep. Finally, she forces herself up to check the time and finds it is already 1:00 p.m. Her quiet day is almost over and all she has done is clean and cry! Her kids will be home from school in less than two hours!

Where would you go if you didn't want your children to know that you played hooky from work – or worse yet, let their attitudes ruin the rest of your day? What would release here from morbid thoughts of murder, divorce and puberty? Shopping, of course!

There was a day when Beverly could shop at a discount store and find socks or a face wash and feel like she was in the lap of luxury.

Now it seems that she can shop for hours and never find what it is she really wants. Whatever it is, it would be much more wonderful if someone else bought it for her. Some people buy extravagant things to feel success and power. All Beverly really wants is to feel appreciated and loved. Because she really doesn't have money to squander, she justifies the trip by deciding that she needs a bulletin board for the kitchen and craft supplies for projects that she will never finish and heads off to the local hobby store.

Her favorite place in the store is the unfinished furniture section where she imagines herself painting small pieces of furniture to embellish her home. She actually has never splurged on a piece, but she enjoys sifting through and admiring the many pieces. Today she spies an interesting wooden chest on the top shelf -- too high for her to reach. Standing on an unfinished stepstool (intended for sale), she struggles to reach the chest.

"It looks like you could use some help!" a man's voice startles her. Turning, she finds herself balancing on a stepstool and looking straight into the eyes of the same stocky, middle-aged man who sat by her at Tania's band concert. Feeling the heat rise in her face, she attempts a coy smile and says "Thanks. I always have troubles getting help here." She perceives a picture of herself looking ridiculously helpless, adding to her embarrassment.

"I don't think this store has any help -- just people to take your money!" the man says in good humor as he reaches the chest down.

Stepping down from the stool, Beverly realizes that this man is not as tall as most and she can make good eye contact with him from the ground. His eyes are a kind, powder blue and what hair he has left is brown. They are probably close in age, but Beverly is sure he looks much older. In recent family photographs, the lighting was bad and Beverly's mouth was full of food, which she knows made her look a lot like her mother; however, she is positive that she looks much younger than that. Was the glance he made at her left hand a sign of that he is desperate? At least she is not desperate!

The next couple of seconds of silence feel uncomfortable, so Beverly begins talking. "Hi, I'm Beverly Scott. I think I sat by you at the concert the other night," she says, faking confidence that almost makes her sound gruff and putting the wooden box that she knows she should not buy casually in her cart.

"Bill Daniels. . . . So, did you enjoy the concert?" he responds.

"Oh, yes! My daughter, Tania, was the oboe soloist." she brags. "What grade is your child in?"

"Melody is a freshman! She lives part-time with her mother, but she and I share a love of music."

"How lucky for her! My X-husband doesn't really keep track of what the kids do in school."

"Really? You know, I've been looking for someone to go to the school musical with. Are you planning to go? I mean . . . if you are not going with someone else . . ." His ears burn as he realizes he does not even know if she is single.

"Actually, I was going to take my boys, but if you would like to join us, we could all go together," Beverly replies, not really knowing why she said that.

"Which show are you going to?"

Beverly had not thought of that and without the schedule, does not even know the dates. "I haven't decided, yet."

"Tell you what; I will give you my phone number and when you decide which show you are going to attend, call me, OK?" He circles his phone number on a business card. The company name on the card is IPS, a local technology contractor.

Beverly is not clear if this is a casual request for company or a date, but she answers confidently, "Sure. That would be fun. I'll call you after I talk to my boys."

"OK. See you around!" Bill waives his hand as he walks away. "Bye!"

In today's world it does not matter, but right now Beverly wishes that she had whipped out her phone number first. That way Bill could be the one to decide whether to call or run. After all, would Shakespeare's story have come out the same if Juliet had awkwardly climbed up to Romeo's balcony? Well, I guess that story did have a morbid ending anyway.

Bill's looks do not fit her expectations of a "Prince Charming", but his kind eyes arouse a longing in her for companionship. What would happen if he loved her through thick and thin, just as she was, forever and ever, Amen? Perhaps she should rethink her expectations.

* * * * *

Late that night, Beverly takes the lovely pine box that she was not going to buy and begins painting it with bright sunflowers, butterflies, and daisies. How she longs for the garden she paints, flowing from her like poetry! It takes four hours to paint, but at a little past one o'clock in the morning she cannot stop looking at it. Finally, she carefully places it on her dresser, slides into bed, says a little prayer, and slips off to sleep.

Chapter 6: Making the Phone Call

On the evening of the third night since her encounter with Bill, Beverly is working at the kitchen sink, preparing salad vegetables for dinner. Her children are light-heartedly teasing one another in the living room and Beverly relishes the pleasant moment.

The kids' good spirits hold out and the family enjoys a good meal together, partaking in enjoyable, claptrap conversation. Afterwards, the boys rummage through their book bags half-heartedly and do very little homework before they hit the remote control; Tania goes to her room to call a friend; and after clearing the table and stacking dishes in the dishwasher, Beverly realizes that it is now or never. After all, it would be rude not to call Bill after she said that she would.

From her cell phone, she can hear one, two, three, four, five rings before an answering-service message comes on. She quickly hangs up the phone, feeling extremely relieved and wondering if she will ever see Bill again to be embarrassed for not calling. As she departs to the living room with the phone in her hand, the phone rings.

Flustered, she answers, "Hello?"

"Hi, this is Melody. Did someone from there call? My dad didn't answer the phone."

"Don't tell me you went through all the trouble of doing a 'last-call-return'," I tease her nervously.

"Yes. Who is this?"

"This is Beverly Scott and I was calling your dad."

"Oh! I'm sorry. Would you like to talk to him?" Her high-pitched voice speaks of her youth as well as remorse.

"Sure," Beverly answers, feeling that "yes" would seem too anxious and wondering if she should have just used the 'wrong number' strategy.

"Hello," Bill answers in a voice that tells her that she definitely should have used the 'wrong number' strategy.

"Hello Bill. This is Beverly Scott. We met at the high school concert and again at the hobby store the other day and you mentioned that you might want company at the school musical." She did not mean to speak so fast.

"Oh! Hi! How are you? I'm sorry – I thought this was another sales call. What show were you planning to go to?" Bill responds with accelerated speech.

"Well, we were thinking about the Wednesday evening show -- but we can probably attend any of them." Beverly could kick herself – why did she leave him the choice? She already promised the kids that they would go on Wednesday!

Bill laughs nervously, "I'll probably go to more than one. Sure, Wednesday is fine. Where shall we meet?"

Beverly's motherly instincts say that she doesn't know this man very well and probably should not tell him where she lives. But he did tell the truth about the daughter. Perhaps he is safe.

Bill interrupts her thoughts, "I have to take Melody early, so maybe we could meet at the school."

"Yes, I'll have to take Tania early and will have the boys with me. Should we meet outside the door at about 6:30?"

"Sure. . . . Well . . . I guess I'll see you there, OK?"

"OK."

"Bye!"

"Bye . . ."

Beverly is relieved the call is over, but worried about how it went. Why didn't she say more? Where was her confidence? Turning off the TV that the boys have now deserted, she retreats to her bedroom and catches a glimpse of herself in the dresser mirror. The night light makes her look fat with tired, worn eyes; but if she holds her mouth just so and tips her chin slightly upward, tucks in her tummy and stands up straight, she can still see the woman she believes she is. Looking a little closer, she wonders what others see. What did Bill see?

'Why do I care? He's probably just being nice. He isn't Prince Charming and might be a beast. He was probably very shocked that I called after he brushed me off at the hobby store and wondered how he could weasel out of meeting me at the kid's show. What a fool I was to call!' Again, she wishes she would have given him her number and left him with the dilemma of whether or not to call.

Long after the kids have gone to sleep, Beverly lies wide awake in bed, unable to rest her mind long enough to fall asleep. Realizing that she could lay awake for hours, she heads out to the piano in the dining room and plays a couple simple songs (because she never really learned to play very well).

The notes ring out clearly with a slight echo in the empty room, symbolizing to her a longing for companionship and love in a world that seems cold and unfeeling. She knows that God must hear her, so she plays awhile, until she finally feels the call of sleep, a little after 1:00 a.m. (again!).

She returns to her bed to lie awake a while longer, wondering why her ex-husband did not love her anymore (or if he ever did) and if men find her attractive at all. Slowly she finally drifts off to sleep.

In her dreams she finds herself a child in the caress of her parents' home with her two brothers and sister celebrating Christmas as though the happiness and love will never end. She admires the brightly lighted Christmas tree, lights and ornaments until her gaze reaches the space where the presents should be. There she sees a dead woman staring at her with eyes wide-open, her dead finger pointing accusingly straight at her.

Chapter 7: Big Date with a Geek

The alarm clock screams its warning with an obnoxious buzz and Beverly wakes up feeling dazed and tired. The wrinkle in her mattress cover is hurting her hip and an earring has drilled a hole behind her ear. The princess who found the pea could not possible be as sensitive to pain as Beverly is this morning. After managing the pain, she rushes downstairs to wake the kids and each one barks back their personal protest.

After the divorce, Beverly's therapist told her that she should let her children get themselves up or suffer the consequences if they were late for school. Unfortunately, the consequences would be that they would not go to school at all, which would be OK with the boys; however, Tania would miss the social contacts. This situation would last until Social Services got word and charged Beverly with child neglect. The "consequence" theory for children is only a therapist's fantasy.

Just thinking about her therapist conjures up acute irritation. Beverly would say, "My ex-husband makes me feel so worthless."

The therapist would reply, "No. You make yourself feel worthless. No one can make you think or feel anything but yourself."

"But he is doing . . . which makes me look like a fool."

"He is making himself look like a fool. The only person who can make you look like a fool is yourself."

"But, he keeps trying to make me mad."

"He is only making himself mad."

Back and forth they would go with these absolutely ridiculous conversations in long one-hour sessions with a grandfather clock ticking out each second of each minute meticulously in the background. When Beverly finally got what the therapist was trying to convey, it changed her life – although the thought of ever being interrogated by a psychologist again makes her all the more anxious to solve her own problems. Maybe that was the point.

Work starts with an early morning meeting. As the meeting drawls on, Beverly vows to devote the rest of her day to a huge ad campaign that started out as just one ad, but now has ballooned into magazine, newspaper and Web ads. She feels relieved that the "creative" aspect of her project is now complete. Although she finds personal creativity invigorating, she finds that collective creativity (bringing several creative people into consensus) is like trying to keep snakes in a shallow terrarium with no lid. After the meeting, she quietly collects endorphins as she checks off the remaining tasks toward completion of her ad campaign.

In a late afternoon meeting, her mind meanders off to what she should wear to Tania's musical tonight. Will Bill really be there or will he ditch her? *Maybe I'll leave work a little early to put on a little extra makeup and perfume . . . Why am I thinking about this? A middle-aged man pays me a little attention and I start having fantasies about Ever After! . . . I wonder what he does for a living and what he would think of my lazy kids. His daughter sounded sweet – or was I deceived? Will he see my kids as awful or understand they are having a tough time? What would it be like to have two incomes in the family again? I don't believe I just thought that!'*

"Beverly?"

Beverly realizes she has just been asked a question. "I'm sorry. Would you repeat the question?"

"Do you think we need the extra capacity of the copier model 4000?"

"If our goal is to save the company money, then we should take into consideration what we pay each individual for the time they spend filling up paper trays. For many of us, that cost is more than $30 an hour. I believe that the company's money could be better spent on other tasks and that we should go for the smaller overall cost of the extra-capacity print tray."

Beverly's years in business have paid off. She realizes how good her "fake" really was when everyone agrees whole-heartedly and the managers give the administrative assistants their blessing to order a fancy new copier.

After the meeting, Beverly returns to her desk where there is a message on the answering machine from Detective Simmons. *'I have already told them everything I know!'* Beverly fumes inside as an infinitesimal flicker of Ellen's dead face crosses her mind. She jots down the number on a sticky note and places it on the side of her phone, but she does not intend to return the call.

* * * * * *

Coats, books, potato chip bags and candy wrappers litter the house when Beverly finally arrives home that evening, but she ignores it all as she throws pizza into the oven for dinner and sets the timer.

After reminding the boys to brush their teeth and Tania to put on her orchestra uniform, Beverly retires to her bedroom to primp, feeling guilty for not asking the kids if they did their homework. Staring at the mirror, she wonders how she is going to look ten years younger, polished and absolutely fascinating in less than twenty minutes.

She fumbles through the bureau drawers and finds a facial masque that she bought two years ago. Smearing it on her face, she not only hopes that it will leave her with a girlish complexion, but also provide the relaxed feeling that she needs to over-ride her overactive nervous system. Looking around for a place to relax, she decides the tub is the best place and starts up the water.

Just as she eases herself into the tub, she hears Tania yelling through the door, "Mom? **MOM!**"

"What?"

"I can't find my black shoes!"

"They are in the hallway closet." Beverly slides deeper into the tub, trying to let go of tension.

"Mom? **MOM!**"

Beverly pretends not to hear.

"MO-OM! Mom! MOM!"

Turning off the water, Beverly shouts back, **"WHAT?!"**

"It's time to go! What are you doing?"

"You don't have to be there until 6:30!"

"But, I promised Jessica that I would be there early!"

"We'll be there at 6:30."

"Great! I told her I would be there early!"

Now Beverly can hear the boys scuffling around in the living room and a huge thud, like something has been knocked over. Closing her eyes and putting her hands over her ears, she tries once more to steal away, but bliss just does not come. Splashing off the face mask, she pulls the plug.

If you could look into Beverly's closet, you would think she must have spent a fortune on clothes. The reality is that she keeps three

47

sizes of clothes – small, medium, and large. Most of her life she has worn the small sizes and she has years of investment there. However, right before her ex-husband left, she swelled up to the medium sizes and then the shock of his leaving put her back into the small sizes. Numbness and bereavement swelled her to the larger sizes after the divorce was final, and now she is in-between medium and large.

The in-between size is frustrating, because she has trouble feeling comfortable in any of her clothes. After digging around, she settles for a casual top that is just a little low in the front – in case she might like this guy more than she anticipates. Sweating profusely from going from a hot tub to a bra and shirt, she looks in the mirror and decides to wear her purple, jewel-neck sweater instead. She does not have the confidence to show off cleavage today.

All that is left of the pizza is crumbs, but Beverly is too nervous to eat anyway. She announces to the kids that it is time to go and they argue all the way to the car over who gets to ride shotgun. Tania wins, because she is wearing her orchestra outfit.

As the embers settle, Snow White takes the driver's seat and leaves for Cinderella's ball with her three teenage trolls. When she arrives, she stands tall with a demure look on her face, waiting for the beast. What if he doesn't come? What if he recognizes the beast in her? Beverly's oldest son, Jason, shoves Mark, causing a domino-effect and nearly knocking Beverly off her heels.

"What are you guys DOING?" she demands loudly, looking up just in time to see Mr. Bill Daniels on the school steps with a hand raised in a graceful wave. The look on Beverly's face is not that of a princess, but she acknowledges him with her eyes and a half-hearted wave. He puts his hand down and Beverly tries to yell out (in an attractive voice of course) over the crowd, "Hi!"

"Who the heck is that?" Jason asks amused.

Beverly conveniently never told the kids that she was meeting Bill. Perhaps she was afraid he would not show up – but there he is, looking like his bubble bath worked out much better than hers. "Just a man I met at Tania's last concert. We'll probably sit by him."

"What a geek!" Tania says with disgust.

If Beverly had three wishes right now, she would wish that she had not brought the boys, looked ten years younger and Bill did not look like a geek. Without the three wishes, she bravely forges on to face what might be a very uncomfortable situation. The boys continue to bop each other as Tania runs off ahead to be with her friends.

48

"Hi, Bill."

"Hi."

"These are my boys, Jason and Mark."

Bill ignores the boys' antics and formally shakes hands with each. Caught off guard, they each sober up and stand a little taller. The little group walks into the building together, feeling like people at a party who have just been introduced, trying not to look like geeks.

They each take a program at the door and Beverly, true to form, drops hers. She makes a clumsy pickup, squinting with her neck twisted in an awkward, up-turned position to make very sure that Bill's chin is safely out of the way.

They quickly find seats near the center of auditorium where Bill and Beverly try, very hard, to carry on light conversation while the boys banter back and forth. Relief from embarrassment comes when darkness envelopes the room. Slowly the curtain rises, revealing a place where people wear colorful costumes and sing passionately whenever they have the opportunity.

There is an oboe in the orchestra that plays flawlessly with such a striking tone that it rings out above all the other instruments. Beverly watches the shadow of her beautiful daughter with intent eyes. For Beverly, she is the dancer, the singer, the show. As a mother she chastises her, but as her audience she is her greatest admirer.

* * * * *

Deep purple, pink, and blue lights slowly dim as the curtain comes down on the first act. The light changes so quickly that the audience feels as though they are awakening from a deep sleep. Conditioning herself again for real life, Beverly has to face that she is sitting next to a man she barely knows and obligated to chitchat.

"Would you like a coke and some popcorn?" Bill asks standing up and stretching.

"That would be great!" Beverly responds, digging through her purse for change.

"I got it."

"Are you sure?"

"Yep. Diet or regular?"

"Diet," Beverly responds, wishing that she had said "regular" so that he would not perceive that she was on an eternal diet.

Bill invites the boys to come with him, leaving Beverly alone, which is a relief, because she needs to use the restroom. There is a long line outside the women's room, but when she finally gets a stall, she sits on the toilet and frantically digs through her purse for cash. She didn't think about snacks for the boys and feels Bill should not foot the entire bill. Ever notice how pennies, nickels and dimes rarely add up to enough to buy anything?

She flushes and heads out to wash her hands, resigned that she does not even have a dollar to offer Bill. While she is at the sink, she takes a quick peep in the mirror and is mortified to see her hair has frizzed out! As dozens of young girls with tight bellies primp next to her, she finger combs her hair, adding a bit of water to get it to stay. Feeling very dowdy among all these young girls, she quickly dries her hands and heads back to find out if her boys are doing anything to embarrass her.

Clumsily climbing through the line of chairs, dodging people and personal artifacts, Beverly finds her boys and Bill conversing with big grins on their faces, each with a huge popcorn and coke. As she wrestles with whether or not to offer to pay Bill back, she takes the last big step to get back to her seat, squeezing between two groups of people who seem to mind greatly. To make it worse, she slips a little and nearly sits in a woman's lap. Trying to appear unflustered, Beverly flops back into her seat and says entirely too quickly, "Oh, goodness! Do I owe you anything?" Her face is beet red.

"Oh no! Glad to share," Bill responds, handing her a diet coke and offering her popcorn.

"The talent in this school is amazing!" Beverly says, realizing that her follow-on comment sounds a bit ridiculous after her clumsy entrance. What a relief it is to Beverly when the lights begin to dim and curtains rise to take everyone back to those colorful costumes, singing conversations, and finally (sigh), happy-ever-after . . .

* * * * *

After the show, Beverly gives the boys her car keys so they can warm up the car while she and Bill wait outside for their girls. She blinks a little prayer that the boys will not turn the radio up too loud or otherwise make a spectacle of their selves.

The two parents exchange comments about how good the show was and make polite conversation as they wait. Beverly tries not to look at Bill's balding head and big belly and wonders if he is making the same concessions for her.

"Tell me, would you like to have dinner some night?" Bill pulls out of nowhere.

"Sure. Do you have a night in mind?" Beverly answers, only to think to herself, *'Oh, great. A geek is asking me out to dinner! The kids will never let me live it down!'*

"How about Saturday night at about 6:30? Do you like Italian? I know a great place."

"Sure. Shall we meet there?"

"Well, we could, but wouldn't it be better if we carpooled?"

"Sure. Let me give you my address." Beverly responds, looking for a pen and paper in her purse. After all, how dangerous can a middle-aged geek who goes to his daughter's concerts be?

Chapter 8: Suspect #1

It's hard to hide from an astute detective like Detective Simmons. Beverly tries to be accommodating, but cannot think of any embellishment that will change the cold, hard facts that the woman is dead and she found her in the woman's bathroom. Her fear kept her from noticing many details and the elapse of time seems to have fogged her memory more. The most baffling question that the detective keeps asking is if she saw the victim's wedding ring. Why the heck would anyone notice a wedding ring on a dead woman?

Jennifer eagerly takes every opportunity to tell Beverly details about Bob's family life. His wife's name was Ellen and they have a son and a daughter, ages four and six. They were planning to go on a cruise the very week of her murder to celebrate their tenth anniversary.

It is not hard to figure out that Jennifer gets most of her scoop from Mary, who seems to know everything about everybody, especially Bob, with whom she is totally infatuated. In the past several months Beverly has heard Mary speaking to the obviously-married Bob many times in a calculated, saccharin-sweet voice that is a dead give-away that she aspires for his affection.

Mary's career at *Gerry's Socks & Shoes* (which started out as Bob's secretary) seems to have advanced far beyond her intellect or talent. She was recently promoted to Lead Administrative Assistant or "Office Manager" as many might describe her duties. Many people feel that she was the least fitted candidate for the position. There is scuttlebutt about who she had to sleep with to get the promotion. Most people believe that Bob was too devoted to his wife ("too nice of a guy") to have an affair with Mary, but others are not too sure.

Beverly cautiously stops off at the downstairs bathroom and notes that there are three other ALIVE people seated in the stalls. Waiting for her turn, she decides to wash her hands. Mary exits one of the stalls, they acknowledge each other and Beverly admits in a hushed tone, "I just don't like to use the bathroom upstairs anymore."

"Me neither. I can't even imagine how you feel having found her dead!"

"I'm not very brave, believe me. Finding her still haunts me."

The toilet flushes and the freckle-faced, sandy-haired woman who has the desk closest to the upstairs bathroom comes out.

"Hi," Beverly greets her.

"Hello," she replies curtly.

"Hi Anna! What are you doing here?" Mary oozes.

"Just happened to be downstairs," Anna responds.

Beverly notices that her face is flushed and she appears upset. Call it a woman's intuition or whatever you want, but suddenly Beverly feels very cold. Anna's desk is right outside the upstairs bathroom. Suppose she was waiting for someone, watching over her cubicle wall until she saw Ellen enter the bathroom. Could she have killed her without getting caught? Anna is a tall woman in good physical shape, probably in her early thirties, more handsome than pretty. She dresses well. If Bob were having an affair, would it be with her?

Thinking becomes an exhausting sport that day for Beverly as she contemplates the murder, the detective's interview and Anna's look on her face in the bathroom. By the time the Friday workday is over, she is relieved to be driving home. As she drives up the driveway, she notices that the garage door is already opening up for her.

Jason greets her with an unusually cheery welcome, "Hi, Mom."

Because Jason is not often away from the remote control, Beverly tries not to act too astonished. "Hi, Honey. How was your day?"

"Fine."

Then she remembers what day it is and cannot stop herself from asking the question that she knows he dreads, "Did you get your report card today?"

He reaches in his pocket, "Yep." As he gives it up, he adds "I know it's not perfect, but I passed everything."

The report has four "C's" and two "D's." Now, Beverly is expected to say something positive, but she knows her son is capable of so much more, so she begins a sentence that is bound to destroy the moment, "Well, passing is good, but you are capable of so much more . . ."

"I knew you'd say that!" Jason snaps as he quickly turns and heads back into the house.

"Wait a minute, Jason. Come here and talk to me a little bit," Beverly pleads.

"Why, so you can yell at me?"

"No. Actually . . . I'd like a hug."

Jason stops in his tracks and stiffens as Beverly walks over gives him an awkward hug. She wants him to know that she loves him and believes in him, but cannot find the words or contain her tears.

"You know, Mom," Jason says consolingly, "I have been doing a lot more homework. I want to graduate from high school. I just don't want to spend all of my time doing schoolwork."

"Jason, I really see that you are doing much more than I thought you were, but what you do in high school affects how much opportunity you will have as an adult!"

"Mom, when I decide what I really want to do, I will make sure that I do what I need to do to get there. There will be a lot of life after high school. I promise that I will graduate, OK?" Jason says, his eyes pleading for understanding.

"OK." Beverly says, noticing how much he looks like his father. "I love you, Jason."

"I love you, too, Mom."

Beverly leans against the car for a moment, savoring the maturity of her son. He's right. There is a lot of life beyond high school.

Chapter 9: Common Ground with a Geek

The marathon of trying on clothes has caused profuse sweat to drench Beverly's face and private parts, sabotaging the effects of her shower. Franticly she settles for the generic look of black pants with a beige short-sleeved blouse and races over to the mirror to remove hot rollers from her hair.

Studying her eyes, she wonders if she should try to perk them up with makeup, but then she remembers that the last time she wore makeup she was aghast to see herself reflected in a restroom mirror with large pools of black mascara under her eyes. She decides against the eye makeup and finishes up with a little blush and lipstick.

The doorbell rings as she is raking a brush through her hair that outgrew its cut two weeks ago. She hears Mark let Bill in, so she pauses a few moments to take one last look in the mirror with her chin held high to one side and mouth held just so. Then she leaves her bedroom to find Bill wearing a similar outfit and standing in the entryway. Mark, who is now back in the living room yelling at a video game character, left Bill there to fend for himself.

"Hi. I'm sorry I'm running a little late. Let me go tell the kids we are leaving," Beverly apologizes.

When Bill and Beverly finally settle in his car, they cannot get past nervous and awkward conversation. Their ridiculous (but polite) ritual continues until their labor abruptly ends in the restaurant parking lot when their focus turns to finding a parking space in the crowded lot. Their plight twists to a welcome comedy as they drive around the building three times before someone finally empties a space that is close enough for them to capture.

Bill made a reservation, so it does not take long to be seated. The inviting fragrance of garlic and home-baked bread permeates inside the restaurant, allowing a bit of tranquility to seep between the two as they take their seats across from each other at the table.

On the walls are large, black and white photographs of generations of happy Italian families doing all sorts of interesting things, from baking bread to dancing. Around the artwork are funny sayings and colorful props.

Bob and Beverly agree on red wine and Beverly starts a new conversation, "Tell me, Bill. What do you do for a living?"

"I'm the Director of Marketing for an electronics engineering company."

"Really? I'm in marketing, too, but I'm just a product manager."

"You probably have more fun than I do! My job is to oversee everyone else having all the fun!"

"Fun? All we ever get to do is attend meetings! Creativity is what we aspire to do when our endless in-boxes are empty!" Beverly jokes.

Together they enter a common world and finally, their souls slowly begin to dance. Long after dinner they are still engrossed in conversation about marketing, kids, and what they hope to do in the future. Their creative hearts sing in harmony, while the candle on the table dwindles down to a smattering of liquid wax.

The waitress has stopped asking if they need anything, the bill has been paid and the duo knows that their night must end. For a few more delicious minutes they sit quietly and then Beverly confides, "I am so glad we had this evening. I have really enjoyed your company. I have not had this much fun in ages."

"Me, too. It has been a great ending for a great week."

"Actually, I've been struggling the past three weeks."

"Why do you say that?"

"You are not even going to believe this, but I found a dead body in the woman's restroom at work three weeks ago last Tuesday. Work has not been the same since."

"What?"

"I'm not kidding. Three weeks ago, I went to the ladies' room and found a woman who had been murdered. I have been totally harassed with questions and carry this horrible picture of her in my mind . . ." Beverly's composure completely falls apart, her voice quivers and tears fall.

"Are you OK?"

"Yes." Beverly's dries her tears with her napkin, fully embarrassed that she has ruined the night with an emotion leak. "It's just been a tough memory to carry."

"I bet! Did you know the woman?"

"No, but she is the wife of one of the directors. It is all so bizarre. It makes me wonder if there is someone I know who is a murderer."

"Is there a suspect?"

"I don't think so." Her eyes are swelling from the coarse linen napkin, but now she knows that she made the right decision to leave off the eye make-up.

Bill reaches across the table to take Beverly's hand. "Boy, you have been carrying a heavy load! I hope tonight made it a little better."

"Honestly, I've ruined the mood, haven't I? I liked it better when we were laughing," replies Beverly, half-laughing and half-crying. For a few seconds, they look at each other and then she adds, "I guess we should call it a night, eh?"

"I think we are lucky they have not thrown us out. Ready to go?"

They head out the door and return to small talk in the car. Finally he says, "Do you like art and craft shows?"

"Yes . . ."

"Would you like to go to the one downtown next weekend?"

"That would be fun!" she replies, musing to herself: '*Did I just make another date with a geek? What does it mean when you have so much in common with a geek?*'

Chapter 10: Mary

On his hands and knees, four-year-old Ivan roughly pushes his cars around using the reflection of the window as his "road." Mary watches with a bored expression on her face, slumped on the couch, wearing a huge Sea Hawks jersey with blue jeans. Her small figure looks child-like for her thirty-five years. Some people would not recognize her at home where she does not make up her face or wear revealing cleavage.

"Mom, I'm coming in for a landing! Here I come!" Ivan races the car across the floor noisily and runs it up the sofa, hitting her foot on purpose.

"Cars don't land." Mary says with obvious boredom.

"Yes, they do! I'm landing on your knee!" he says, landing the car on her knee.

Mary pushes him away and goes to the kitchen to get coffee.

"Mom, are we doing anything today?" Ivan asks.

"I'm waiting for a phone call."

"From your BOYFRIEND?"

"I don't have a boyfriend right now. WHAT ARE YOU DOING?"

Ivan is pushing the car up the kitchen wall in short strokes, making metal grey marks on the wall. "I'm flying!"

"Cars do not fly! Now get it off the wall!"

Ivan does not stop, so Mary lunges toward him and grabs his hand. "Stop it!" she says with aggravation.

"I was just playing!" Ivan answers, his large brown eyes meeting hers and his little mouth pulled into a pout. Mary is softened, but the phone rings.

"Hello . . . No, I was just playing with Ivan. How are you?"

Ivan goes back to running the car up the wall, but Mary is oblivious. "Today? . . . Well, I will have to find a babysitter . . . Are you sure you don't mind? . . . OK . . . I'll bring him. See you in a while, OK? Bye!" Out of the corner of her eye, she sees Ivan marking up the wall.

"IVAN! You didn't listen and look what you did!" she screams. Ivan runs like a fugitive to his bedroom.

"Ivan, you need to listen to Mommy!" Mary tries to convince him as she chases after him. He has already grabbed his blanket and flung it over his head where he is sucking his thumb and rubbing the blanket nervously. "We are going to lunch with Cindy, do you remember her?"

"I don't like Cindy. She's mean."

"I'll get you a toy if you're good. Would you like that?"

"I want to stay home!"

"Well, we are going, so you get clean clothes on while I get ready, OK?"

"OK."

When Cindy finally drives up the driveway, Ivan runs in to tell his mom, who is primping.

"Why aren't you changed?" Mary demands.

"I'm getting ready!" Ivan yells over his shoulder nervously as he runs back to his room.

Mary answers the door. "I'm sorry, Ivan isn't ready. Have a seat and he'll be ready in a minute."

From her perch on the couch, Cindy can hear Ivan protesting loudly. She goes to the hallway mirror and teases her bangs up which she feels make her look like a rock star. At work she has to tie her hair back, but when she goes out she likes to let it go wild – and wild it is with her frizzy natural curls. Even with the streaks of natural gray, she feels it is her best trait. Short and stocky and about ten years older than Mary, Cindy obviously is not aware that styles have changed since she was in high school.

Soon Mary and Ivan come out with Ivan looking pretty spiffy, except that his hair sticks out like a wild child.

"Hi, Ivan. How are you? I have a comb. Do you want me to comb your hair?" Cindy baby talks, but Ivan backs away.

"I don't want you to do it!" he protests. "I want Mom to."

"Let's just go. I've been fighting with him all morning." Mary says.

As they proceed to the door, Cindy reaches for Mary and kisses her on the cheek. Mary pulls away.

"You know," Cindy says in a low voice, "You are beautiful."

"Cindy, I told you before. I really like being your friend, but that is all I want to be right now."

"I guess I just hope you will change your mind."

Ivan chimes, "I thought we were going to eat! I'm hungry!"

Cindy replies "Come on, Sweetie. Auntie Cindy will feed you. I heard you have been bad today, though. You need to be nicer to your mom."

Ivan stays as far from Cindy as he can and holds his mother's hand firmly.

Cindy says, "Ivan, someday you will be glad your mom is pretty. It has its advantages, wouldn't you say, Mary?"

Mary's mood changes as she giggles, "To be sure!"

"Do you have your ring?"

"Yes. I brought another one, too. I think that together they would make a fantastic pair of earrings!"

"Cool! I have a huge sapphire that Amy gave me years ago. I'm going to have it made into a pendant. If I ever see her again, I'll flash it at her!"

"I never thought anything would mend a broken heart, but you are right, making new jewelry out of gifts from ex's is sweet revenge!"

"See! It grows on you, doesn't it?"

The two women giggle, but Ivan's little face is wrinkled as he quick-steps to keep up.

Mary looks back at him, "Ivan, are you ok?"

"Yes," Ivan says defiantly fighting to keep up.

Mary stops in her tracks. "Where would you like to eat, Ivan?"

Finally caught up, he takes her hand. "I don't know."

"It's your choice, ok?"

"I want to go home."

Mary's face falls and she looks at Cindy, "I'm sorry, Cindy. Ivan has had a really bad day and I think I should take him home."

"Oh nonsense," Cindy retorts. "Come on Ivan. We can eat wherever you want!"

"I want to go home," Ivan repeats.

"We'll go another day, Cindy. Honest, Ivan and I just need to go home today. Come on Ivan!"

Cindy is miffed, but she responds, "Do want me to come?"

"If you like peanut butter and jelly!" Mary responds.

"Nah. I'll talk to you later, ok?"

"Are you sure?"

"Yes. Peanut butter is not my favorite food."

"OK. Call me later, ok? Bye!"

"Good bye! Good bye, Ivan, you SPOILED BRAT!"

"Good bye," Ivan responds waving, content now that he is going home with his mother. They head back to their house to make peanut butter and jelly sandwiches, play video games and watch an animated movie with popcorn.

As Ivan drifts off to sleep that night, Mary cannot help but realize that he is the best thing she has in her life right now. She knows her family does not approve of her lifestyle and really wants a stable family for Ivan, but it seems to her that every time she believes she has found the right person to share her life, that person turns out to be totally wrong. Ivan's father was very violent and what was confusing was that he was so NICE to her before she married him.

Her last two relationships also ended violently and she wound up in the hospital after one of the beatings. Included in her many relationships were several happily married men. It was Mary's theory that if she could nab an existing and proven good husband and father, he would somehow become her happily married man and a great father for Ivan. It never dawned on her that they weren't good husbands or fathers if they agreed to have an affair.

Mary longs for what she sees others have and sometimes blames Ivan for her lack of luck with relationships. If there is science to choosing a relationship, she certainly has not found the right formula.

Her mother (who often cares for Ivan on weekends so Mary can date) tells Mary that God will punish her if she does not clean up her act. But, Mary does not believe that God would be so cruel as to judge her on bad luck alone. Is it her fault that she attracts all the wrong men or that all the men she picks turn out to be creeps?

As an only child, Mary craves attention and is oblivious to how that one trait affects so many of her choices and sabotages her happiness. In grade school, she was always that sweet little blonde star who worked hard for grades and always did what she was told. No one ever guessed that she maintained her industrious endeavors because she craved the teachers' attention, as well as her fellow students' envy.

By the time she got to high school, she changed her game and played for bigger stakes: popularity and boyfriends. Failing to make cheerleader in the tenth grade was a catastrophic event; however, she did succeed every other year, was Senior Prom Queen, and Valedictorian. At graduation, she gave an excellent speech with perfect poise in her scratchy, child-like voice and everyone loved it.

Smart and savvy as she was, Mary had no aspirations to go to college. She expected to marry young and spend the rest of her days getting manicures and going to parties. She focused on finding men on college campuses, around fancy eating establishments, and at the many parties her parents hosted.

But schemes in her adult years have been challenging. Her first husband was her mother's pick, a lawyer working his first year in a prestigious law firm.

The wedding was absolutely gorgeous in pink tulle, white organza and light green satin. There were swans in the pond, eight bridesmaids and grooms men, a flower girl and ring bearer.

The flower girl and ring bearer looked so cute walking up the aisle together; he in a tuxedo coat with shorts and she in a lacey, light green dress fluffed out with a full slip. They were Mary's cousins; the girl five years old and the boy only three.

Prime rib was on the menu with a lovely salad and fragrant garlic potatoes. Guests admired a five layer white wedding cake with cherry filling and real flowers reflecting the bridal bouquet. Mary's ring was adorned with a large marquis diamond and a full row of diamonds all around. Everything was perfect.

But the wedding slowly faded away and life fell into monotony as Nathen tired of her trite conversation and neediness. While she was pregnant with Ivan, Nathen found a woman that he found more interesting. When Mary found out, she became venomous and they fought often, sometimes getting physical. Mary's mother rescued her when she found out what was going on and her father paid big money to get the best divorce settlement possible for his sweet girl.

Now, after several failed relationships, Mary's parents no longer come to her rescue, which makes her lovers' rejections all the more depressing. She loves Ivan with all her heart, but sometimes he is just another strike against her as she searches for fame, fortune and the perfect mate to no avail.

Chapter 11: Family Ties

Beverly's weekend starts with a Friday night visit with her mother, Rachael, a plump beautiful person who has weathered marriage with a sense of humor, acute intelligence and a mean temper, when appropriate. Her children and grandchildren have treasured memories that only she could have orchestrated. She has very few vices, except that she knows everything. Although her family bears the marks of a matriarch, after more than fifty years her beloved husband still can take down the house with a well-delivered joke.

If Beverly had one wish, it would be to enrich her children's childhood with the caliber of fond memories she attributes to her mother. Her goal was to raise her children exactly like her own mother had (except for the temper) but it was a hopeless and unreachable pursuit. Where Rachael takes on hardships like a wrestling champ, Beverly wrestles with adversity and aspires to fairy tales. Beverly's older sister (Norma) and younger brothers (Joseph and Ned) don't seem to irritate Rachel as much as Beverly does with her head in the clouds.

Beverly listens patiently as Rachel raves about Norma's spectacular children who cleaned her yard last Saturday morning (while Beverly's children were sleeping till noon). Norma's oldest child is on the honor roll and her boy is a soccer star. She and her husband (a bond made in heaven) have started up a maid-service together that is so profitable that they are looking into starting up a franchise.

Beverly chooses not to spoil the mood by enlightening her mother that she found a dead woman in the bathroom and is dating a geek. Instead, she comments with "cool, "neat" and "great," as applicable. The one thing Beverly does not want right now is motherly-advice that always makes her regress from an aspiring career woman to her mother's child. As Rachael drawls on about how Beverly's brother's wife is home-schooling, Beverly wonders if Rachael lives her life through her kids because she was never allowed (or financially able) to live the life she dreamed about.

Rachael married young and never had the opportunity to go to college. In recent years she has had to work as a receptionist at a doctor's office to make ends meet. Her children seem to be her hands and eyes to a world she never experienced. Beverly cannot help but admire her courage as she continues to work in her old age to help keep her household afloat.

Suddenly, Beverly realizes something that interrupts her thoughts for a moment. Perhaps she is more like her mother than she ever thought and possesses a personal courage that is difficult for others to see. Rachael's voice fades into the background as Beverly's thoughts surface. Silently she conveys her message to her mother: *'Don't worry, Mom, when I was in labor with my children, I remembered how brave you said you were, so I did not scream or cry, even when the pain was excruciating and the labor went on for hours. When my husband deserted me, I fought desperately for his love, wanting to keep my fairy-tale family together like you did. When I lost that battle, I struggled to buy my own house, finish my education and care for my kids with a little more than half of the income I once had. When I found a dead woman in the bathroom, I did not let my panic overcome my ability to do the right thing. Even though you believe that I am a weak person who complains and cries too much, I know deep down that I am brave. If I could have only one wish, I would wish that you could see my courage.'*

As her visit ends and Beverly hugs her mother goodbye, she feels a bond that she has never felt before in a sisterhood where individual dreams are not as important as doing the right thing and women are comrades in a world terribly amiss of right. Perhaps her mother would never see the resemblance, but Beverly feels blessed to have seen a glimpse of her mother within herself.

* * * * *

On Saturday morning, Beverly wakes up only a half-hour later than usual. The house is always quiet on Saturdays, because her teenagers sleep in and Mark (who rises early) has no one to banter.

Mark did not talk until he was three -- probably because Tania and Jason always spoke for him and his father did not like conversation unless it was informative or ridiculously funny. Mark was a happy baby with a fetching dimpled smile who could entertain himself for long periods of time. Holding him was simply delicious.

At twelve years old, he swears that his brother and sister always beat him up and his parents neglect him. He often expresses anger towards his father when Beverly is around, but is the first one to run out to see him when he visits. Like all children, he wants to be his father's favorite, but his father is too involved in his new life to consider visitation much more than a chore.

On this particular Saturday, Tania is spending the night with a friend and Jason is still sleeping. Beverly putters around the house for a while, getting dishes caught up and laundry started for the weekend while Mark lays belly-down on the floor, half-heartedly playing a video game. As she wipes her hands on a kitchen towel, she catches site of how bored he looks. "How would you like to go to the movies and lunch with me?" she asks on a whim.

"Right now?" He is game!

"Sure! We could hit the matinee rates and then go to lunch."

"OK!" He abandons his game and goes to look for his shoes.

Beverly knows that she *should* tell him to turn off the game and television, but that would spoil the moment. She quietly turns off the game and the television for him. When he reappears with his shoes, she casually asks (cautiously, playing the parenting game), "After you've washed your face and brushed your teeth, we can go, OK?"

While Mark brushes his teeth, Beverly quickly brushes her hair and checks her appearance in the mirror. When she returns to the living room, she realizes that she should have told Mark to brush his hair, so she makes a risky move, "Would you please brush your hair, too?"

"Why didn't you tell me that in the first place?" Mark grumbles, as though brushing hair is something new.

It would make sense to look at the Internet or the newspaper to find out what movies are playing at what times, but work requires so much planning, forecasting, and rudiment that Beverly likes to be spontaneous in her leisure time. She finds it delectable to dawdle, experiment and adventure.

Tania and Jason used to enjoy Saturday excursions, but now only Mark joins his mom on these suspenseful rendezvous. Beverly cherishes these special moments with her youngest son who has not yet fully embraced that soon he will be a teenager.

The movie house is still closed when they arrive (first movie is not until 10:30 a.m.), so they walk down the street to get coffee, cocoa, and a sinfully sweet cinnamon roll. Beverly starts the conversation, "Who is your favorite teacher?"

"Mr. Stevens."

"He is your science teacher, right? You've always liked science. What are you learning about?"

"Dumb stuff so far. I already know most of it."

"What do you want to learn?"

"I just want to know how everything works."

"You know, Mark, not everything you learn in school is a fact. Sometimes, as scientists find out more and more about what is around us, they find out that what we think we know is false. In some ways, science books should be called 'Science Theory' books. When I was a child, they taught us that the distinction between animals and people was that people could use deductive reasoning and tools, and had language. Now we know that various animals can do at least some of those things."

"So can computers."

"Do you think computers use deductive reasoning or that they are programmed to come to certain conclusions?"

"I think people are programmed to come to certain conclusions."

"Why do you say that?"

"Well, every decision you make is based on what you know or think you know about life. We might all be a bug in a sloth's nose, but if we don't know, then we may think we live in the most beautiful world in the universe."

"Do you think God would put us in a sloth's nose?"

"Well, only if it was the best place for us to grow into what he wants us to be!"

Beverly looks at him admiringly. Perhaps he is not like his dad at all. They go to a kid's action movie, eat double-buttered popcorn with coke and then go out to lunch. Beverly is too full to actually eat lunch, but her growing boy downs a full hamburger. They giggle like school kids and for a while the haunting images of a murder fall into the background as if they were just a bad dream.

Chapter 12: Amateur Blunder

No matter what road you take on a weekend, it always leads back to work on Monday. As Beverly trudges up the stairs, she passes Anna heading down and they acknowledge each other with a formal, "Good morning."

As they pass, Beverly feels an out-of-character urge to go search Anna's cubicle for evidence of murder. She scouts out the hallway and then quietly slips into Anna's cubicle. Not knowing exactly what she is looking for, she begins timidly pulling out desk and file drawers.

Looking up just in time to see Mary striding by, Beverly tries to deter suspicion by grabbing a pencil and pretending to write a note, acutely aware that her face is flushing. Mary, as usual, seems oblivious to anything out of the ordinary, so Beverly continues pulling out the bottom file drawer. Shock hits her like a bullet when she sees a small gun slipped into the front hanging file folder. Panic jabs in quick strokes at her heart as she quickly closes the drawer.

Who should she tell? How would she explain how she found it? Beverly races back to her desk wondering why Nancy Drew would have even thought about entering a haunted house, knowing full well that the very bowels of hell dwelled within. Like a ravenous dog ready to devour every clue, Ms. Drew would forge on until she had unraveled every scrap of an impending mystery. Perhaps she was a masochist.

"Did you need something?" Anna looks annoyed as she approaches Beverly's desk.

"Oh! A . . . Hi, Anna," Beverly answers, feeling faint. "Uh . . . I just borrowed a paperclip. Hope you don't mind!"

"Of course not. Mary just said you were at my desk." She studies Beverly's face and then adds, "Next time, would you ask first?"

"Sure. I was just in a hurry. No problem."

To Beverly's relief, Anna walks off in a huff. Beverly's heart skips one more beat with the ring of her desk phone.

"Hi, Beverly," Mary oozes. "We haven't had lunch in a while – would you like to go to lunch with me today?"

"Hi, Mary." Beverly answers, irritated and baffled over why Mary would be calling her. To understand, you would need to know that two years ago, Beverly, Mary and Jennifer were everyday lunch mates. When the Company reorganized, all of their job titles were changed, but only Beverly got a promotion to management. The promotion seemed fair to Beverly, because only she had a Bachelor's degree; however, Mary and Jennifer were a bit miffed. "I don't know – it's been a busy morning."

"Please! We have not had lunch in so-o-o long!"

"Did you ask Jennifer?"

"No. Jennifer already has plans. Please! We could go 11:30 or 12:00."

"OK. Let's go at 11:30. I need a break."

At lunch, Mary and Beverly make small talk, mostly about Mary. To Beverly, Mary is about as vain and self-centered as one person can be. She left her husband and then took up with a charming younger man who jilted her just a few weeks later. Now she raises her son alone, but is always sleeping with someone. She is absolutely overflowing with gossip, which Beverly sometimes finds entertaining. Mary has come in to work with an occasional bruise on her face, but it does not seem to deter her sexuality or her lifestyle.

"Do you know if there is a suspect for Ellen's murder?" Mary asks casually after a totally unrelated repartee.

"No. It's sure sad, isn't it?"

"Yes. Bob has been really torn up about it."

"Is he back at work today?"

"No. He's staying home with his kids for another week. He's such a good father. He calls in to see how things are going at work."

"I really feel for him. I hope they find the murderer."

"It was probably someone off the street."

"Did you know Anna very well?"

"Why?"

"I don't know. She is so close to the bathroom that you would think she would have seen or heard something."

"She was probably away from her desk, but you are right. It seems weird that no one saw anything. Jennifer said that the cleaning team was cleaning the restroom early that morning, but Tom's admin says they never clean restrooms until evening. I guess it was just a fluke that no one saw anything."

" . . . So how is Ivan?" Beverly changes the subject.

"Oh, he's fine. Doing well in pre-school . . ."

They lose track of time and are late back to work. Beverly is late for her one o'clock phone meeting. Just as she is dialing in, a blood-curdling scream hurls from the hallway. Everyone, including Beverly, drops what they are doing and runs to the hallway. Standing outside the restroom with a transparent look of horror is an elderly administrative assistant, Mona. "She's dead! Anna's dead!" she bawls, shaking profusely.

Beverly's body feels inanimate as she stares at the sea of people hurrying over to comfort Mona and peek in the bathroom. She immediately remembers the gun and wonders if she should have taken some kind of action.

For the next several hours, investigators again turn the ladies restroom into their office. As Beverly leaves for the day, she hears the tense whispers of several women in the hallway. Detective Simmons is with them, standing near the stairway, so Beverly waves at her gingerly. The detective acknowledges the gesture with a half-smile and raised hand, looking very weary.

* * * * *

The long day ends at home with Beverly busying herself in the kitchen, cleaning and putting frozen pizzas in the oven. She knows that she would feel better if she found a different job. Unfortunately, another job with the same pay would not be easy to find and because she "witnessed" the deceased Ellen, the story probably cannot end until someone is brought to trial – if the murderer is ever found. She feels like an ensnared character in a tall tale.

The phone rings and though it startles her, Beverly does not attempt to answer it, because she knows the kids will clamor to get it.

"MOM! The phone's for you!" Tania bellows from her bedroom.

"Hello?" Beverly answers, feeling panic well up her side.

"Hi. How was your day?" It's only Bill, not Prince Charming, but a welcome comfort.

"You don't want to ask," Beverly replies.

"That bad, eh?"

"Another person was found dead in the woman's bathroom today."

"You're kidding, right?"

"I wish I was."

"Oh my gosh! Are you OK?"

"Yes. I didn't know her very well, but she was my suspect for Ellen's murder."

"Hmmm . . . was this lady murdered?"

"I don't know. What upsets me is that I invaded her privacy today and found something I should not have . . ." Guilt keeps her from continuing.

"Are you going to tell me what?" Bill prods.

"It was a gun."

"No way! Did you tell anyone?"

"No, but I think that Anna suspected that I found it."

"Your life is starting to sound like a soap opera. You know, you MUST tell someone about the gun."

"Yes, I already made up my mind to call the detective tomorrow from work."

"Sounds like a plan!"

"So how was YOUR day?"

"I guess kind of boring, compared to yours."

Exhausted from her own thoughts and worries, she turns the subject to him and his world to escape hers. Soon they are so engrossed in conversation that time seems suspended.

"Mom, have you seen my red socks?" Tania interrupts abruptly, standing in the kitchen with her arms crossed.

"I've got to go, too." Bill says. "You have a good night and don't think too much about all this murder stuff. If you need someone to talk to, don't hesitate to call, OK?"

"Thanks." Beverly does not want to say goodbye. Like Christopher Robin, she wants to hold on to her Pooh. Relinquishing the phone, Beverly makes tea and sits quietly in the living room for what seems like a very long time. The boys devour the pizza, but Beverly does not move from her perch. As the night light fades, she reluctantly interrupts her thoughts long enough to tell the kids to brush teeth and go to bed. For the next couple hours, she sits in a daze in the living room, not wanting to confront her fears in the dark of the night. Slowly she drifts off to sleep in her chair.

Chapter 13: Jennifer's Suspicions

"I thought you might call. Let me see . . . I've got a trial that I have to testify for all this week in a court case, so can we meet next Monday?" Detective Simmons sounds completely nonchalant, as if murder is as natural as childbirth.

"OK. I guess so." Beverly answers, a little unsure because she was hoping to get her knowledge of the gun off her chest today. She wonders if she should have told Detective Simmons that it was urgent, but then she convinces herself that the detective probably already knows about the gun, because they surely searched Anna's cubicle in their investigation. She knows that with all the eavesdropping and gossip in the office, it would be best not to tell her about the gun on her office phone.

"Hi, Beverly." Beverly looks up to see Jennifer standing at her desk.

"Hi . . . I missed you at lunch yesterday," Beverly replies, a bit flustered. She makes it clear that she is busy by not looking up and working on straightening her desk.

"Oh? Who did you go with?"

"Mary. She said you already had plans."

"Actually, she didn't ask. I ate at my desk yesterday. Where did you guys go?"

"Just to a fast food." Beverly responds, a little bewildered. "What's up?" she asks, finally looking up to see Jennifer nearly in tears.

"I just wondered if you knew Anna very well . . ."

Jennifer's eyes are puffy, like she has been crying. Seeing her distress, Beverly softens up a bit, "No. I actually just met her formally the other day."

"She and I have been having lunch together . . . This is really hard for me," Jennifer says as she starts to lose her composure.

"I'm so sorry, Jennifer. Do you need some time off?"

"No. I'll be OK."

"The news last night said that she committed suicide – took poison. I just don't think she would do that! It also said that she was missing her wedding ring. Anna had a really beautiful wedding ring with an eternity ring under it that her husband gave her just last week for their fifth anniversary."

"That's odd. The one question the detectives kept asking me when I found Ellen was did she had her wedding ring on. Hey, would you like to have lunch together today? You sound like you need to talk."

"Yes. What time would be good for you?"

"Let me see . . ." Beverly responds, scanning her calendar, "how about 12:15?"

"Sure. I'll see you then, OK?"

"OK."

At 12:22, Jennifer and Beverly are in Jennifer's car, driving to a restaurant.

"I just had to talk to someone . . . Anna and I had become pretty good friends since she began working here," Jennifer begins. "After Ellen's murder, she told me that she needed to talk to me and asked if I would have lunch with her. Then she cancelled lunch saying that she was too busy with a new project. The following day at lunch, she told me that she couldn't remember what she wanted to talk to me about."

"How weird. Do you think she knew something about Ellen's murder?"

"That's my theory. She just had a baby and always talked about her husband like she was madly in love with him. It just does not seem to me like she was unhappy or mentally ill. I really don't think she would have committed suicide."

Beverly states the obvious, "She sits so close the restroom that you would think she would have seen something."

"That's what I think, but why wouldn't she tell the investigators when they questioned her?"

"It seems like she would have . . . unless someone was threatening her."

Jennifer seems relieved that someone shares her theory. The two women talk in hushed tones with teary eyes, trying to puzzle together what they both suspect, but guilt keeps Beverly from telling Jennifer about the gun in Anna's cubicle. What would Jennifer think of her if she knew about this breach of integrity?

Long after lunch, Beverly is still thinking about how she will explain to the Detective how she found that gun. Finally, she leaves a phone message for Detective Simmons saying that she was mistaken about what she had intended to tell her and would not be meeting with her on Monday. The guilt she feels does not overpower her relief.

The crime scene haunts Beverly as she retraces what happened. The motionless Ellen was tall and plump with dark eyes fully open. Her medium-length, dark brown hair was in disarray and she wore a red skirt, nylons, black heels, and a brightly flowered suit coat.

In movies and books, there are always clues. Beverly wonders what she could have missed. Redrawing the scene in her mind, Beverly cannot for the life of her remember the ring, but there was a closed black purse on the floor in front of Ellen with a giant gold clasp.

Why would someone take her ring, but not her purse? Beverly can now see it quite clearly in her head – the purse. As she ponders this clue, she wonders why Ellen did not bang on the walls or make loud panic noises to draw attention. Was she unafraid of her murderer because it was someone she knew -- or did the attack happen so silently and invisibly that she did not know what was happening? What clues were the detectives able to find? How long had she been dead? Could it have happened the night before?

Beverly reaches deep, but she cannot remember any more details of consequence about Ellen, so she begins to rationalize about Anna's death. Anna was found dead at about one o'clock in the afternoon. Women tend to go to the restroom together. If Anna went to lunch with someone, maybe she went into the restroom with her murderer or murderess. Now Beverly has totally freaked herself out as she realizes that the "murderer" was almost certainly a "murderess" and probably someone she knows or at least works with. Well, if Anna was murdered, that is.

Her fingers tremble as she pushes the buttons on her phone. "Hello, Jennifer?" Beverly fakes calm.

"Hello."

"It's me again -- Beverly. This may sound like a strange question, but do you know if anyone went to lunch with Anna yesterday?"

"No. Sure don't."

"OK. I was just curious."

After the fruitless call, Beverly's mind screams: '*The Detective Agency of Beverly Jean Scott is now officially closed! Nightmares desert me and demons of death cease your haunting!*'

Chapter 14: Spring Art & Craft Show

Winter sleet turns to spring monsoons in Seattle, but this April day the sun dazzles the many-colored flower boxes along the downtown streets. The warm fragrance of spring beckons the senses with a mix of salt water, fish and flowers. Banjoes and guitars twang in the distance.

Bill is with Tania and Mark, conversing with a local female artist whose long, blue-gray hair frizzes around a brightly colored scarf. Her thin figure is draped in a sweet, peasant-style dress that betrays her obvious age. Although Bill and Beverly both immensely enjoy these shows, Bill enjoys talking to each artist while Beverly prefers to meander and admire the many artistic treasures in silence, wondering off by herself each time Bill stops to talk.

Bill would like their relationship to go farther, but Beverly just can't get past the feeling that Bill is just a diversion until she finds Prince Charming. He is a comfort that she does not deserve and a delicacy that she can't give up.

The deaths at *Gerry's Sock & Shoes* five months ago are no closer to resolution than they were when they happened. To get their employees back on track, the company spent a small fortune on personal and group therapy. With just a touch of insanity tossed into the stress of daily life, Beverly turned down the Company's offer of personal counseling. She feels that other than the flashbacks and panic attacks in public restrooms, she is bouncing back quite nicely. Surely, the haunting will go away with time.

There have been some changes at work. Jennifer found a job with a different company. She barely said goodbye when she packed up her things. Beverly has not heard from her; however, Mary keeps saying that she has her new phone number. There is a young, quiet blonde with funky purple glasses who sits in Anna's chair now. Beverly often sees Mary baby-talking to Bob in the hallway in that annoying saccharine voice, tossing her hair back with exaggerated panache. The scuttlebutt is that she is being a bit too obvious a little too soon after

Ellen's death, but Beverly knows that Mary lives for the moment and is totally oblivious to what people think.

In Beverly's fantasies, the highly ambitious Bob, with his six-figure income and distinguished looks might take a new look at her in a year or two, rising star in the company; mature, yet still bearing a youthful twinkle in her eyes. Deep down, she knows that he would never take a second glance. Beverly's downfall is her reluctance to play the game.

Is it just a coincidence that she is thinking of Bob and Mary and then recognizes them approaching in the distance? Mary is dressed in a beautiful, gauzy white dress walking beside the handsome Bob. Beverly lifts her hand to waive, but they do not see her. Although Beverly is a bit shocked to see them in public together, she cannot help but notice Mary's implied innocence that radiates as her golden hair blows softly against her sun-kissed face. Who could help but be entranced with her?

A beautiful bouquet of dried flowers offered from behind startles Beverly, but it takes her only a moment to realize it is Bill, his face beaming with pleasure. Tania has a small painted canvas in a frame in her hands, but Mark informs everyone that he doesn't want anything except food, so they decide to go get a bratwurst.

Waiting at the bratwurst stand, Beverly hears that familiar child-like voice from behind, "Hi, Beverly!"

"Mary! How are you?" Beverly says as she turns, noting that Bob is right behind her.

"Bill, this is Mary Zimmerman and Bob Schneider from work." Bill and Bob shake hands and Beverly introduces the kids.

Mary is absolutely glowing. On her neck is a beautiful silver pendant, which causes Beverly to comment, "What a beautiful pendant, Mary!"

"Oh! Thank-you! My grandmother passed away and this is the only thing that she left me. I really love it. You know, my mother never told me who my real father was, so she was my only grandmother. I treasure it so much – it is my only inheritance."

They dine together on a bench and wind up walking through the rest of the fair together. Bill and Bob get along very well and Mary and Beverly are comfortable with each other. It winds up being a very pleasant day for all. When they finally part, everyone is sunburned and tired.

Later that evening, Beverly is quietly weeding through the week's junk mail that clutters the table. Tania sits within a few feet of

Beverly in the living room, admiring her treasures from the show. "Mom, do you think you and Bill will get married?"

"Oh! I don't think so, Tania! We are just very good friends." Beverly tosses off.

"Isn't he your best friend?"

"Yes. I guess he is."

"Well, if I were looking for someone to spend the rest of my life with, I would pick my best friend."

Beverly stops sorting mail and notices that Tania is fondling the small painting of a flowered field that Bill bought her. Feeling her hypocrisy shining out for the world to see (especially her daughter), Beverly' heart fills with self-reproach. How dare she wait for Prince Charming, when she already has the best friend anyone could ever ask for?

Tania continues, "I just think you should not lead him on if you don't want him. He is too nice of a guy."

"Maybe I keep him around because I already know that."

"Would you marry him if he asked you?"

"I really don't know."

They sit in the silence, neither one really knowing how to resolve the conversation. The phone saves them both and Tania runs off to answer it, leaving Beverly alone to wonder if Bill would ever ask her to marry him, and if he did, if she would say, "Yes."

Tall, dark and handsome, Beverly's ex-husband seemed a good friend in the beginning. But time revealed his true self was selfish and self-indulging. If Tania were looking for a mate, Beverly knows she would tell her to look for friendship, interests and shared beliefs. For herself, though, she is looking for a particular box, all tied up in ribbons with everything she is infatuated with inside and a guaranteed forever-after.

Is indelible, unconditional love a fairy tale or just the Prince Charming part? Would Bill love her forever or leave her loving him and wondering why? Perhaps the pain of a love lost works like the Pavlov's dog trick. You can avoid the possibility of the excruciating pain of love lost by finding an unending supply of excuses not to commit to anyone, even though your soul is desperately crying out for companionship. Beverly wonders if she is sabotaging her own destiny. Who else should you marry but your best friend? The question hangs in the air accusingly.

Chapter 15: Mary's Big Fat Lie

When long, hot summer days finally yield to falling leaves, *Gerry's Socks & Shoes* always has a dinner-dance at an elegant hotel where they entertain Board members and psych up employees for the crucial winter holiday strategies. Because Bob is the only person in the company besides Beverly that Bill knows at the affair, he naturally steers her towards Bob and Mary. Beverly is slow to follow, as she attempts to acknowledge each person she knows along the way.

Mary's overly dressy, backless pink formal looks absolutely breathtaking with her gorgeous necklace and earring set, covered with stones that sparkle like diamonds. On her left hand is an obnoxiously-large engagement ring. Although the dress code was clearly business attire, Beverly feels extremely underdressed in her navy suit and heels next to Mary. Bill and Bob go to get drinks.

"Is that an engagement ring?" Beverly teases Mary with a twinkle in her eye.

"Yes! Isn't it beautiful? I'm so excited! Bob and I plan to marry in January!"

"Oh! I'm so happy for you! Congratulations!" The words are counterfeit, but Beverly knows Mary will not interpret them that way.

"Thanks. I know it seems kind of early since his wife's death, but people need to put the past in the past."

"Yes, and it's never too soon to love again," Beverly agrees, biting her tongue.

"We are going on a Caribbean cruise for our honeymoon. I am so excited!"

"Oh, that should be fun!"

Bill and Bob come back to the table with drinks and the conversation turns to other things. An absolutely divine meal featuring pepper-crusted salmon steak or lemon chicken is served. Before dessert (and speeches), Mary and Beverly take off for the restroom together, which is extremely crowded. As they wash their hands and primp, Beverly comments to Mary how beautiful her necklace and earrings are.

"I feel a little overdressed," Mary admits.

"You look beautiful. I love rhinestones!"

"Oh! But they're diamonds!" She protests.

"Wow! -- Did you get them from Bob?"

"A . . . no . . . My grandmother left me her rings and I had these custom-made out of the stones . . ." Her eyes meet Beverly's and immediately she sees that Beverly is not buying the story.

Fear flushes Beverly's face as she finds herself thinking about two murdered women who were missing rings and a silver pendant that Mary said was her only inheritance from her grandmother. She can hardly breathe. "Well, we'd better get back to the men," she says, trying to hide her elevated blood pressure.

"Wait . . ."

Beverly turns to see that Mary has turned white as a sheet. "Are you OK?" Beverly asks, trying to hide her own fear.

"What are you thinking?" Mary demands.

Beverly tries to be coy. "About your jewelry? I think it is beautiful! Let's go see if our dessert has been served, OK?" Now the crowded room is emptying and only two women remain primping, so Beverly quickens her step. Mary closely follows with no more comment.

For Beverly, the night now burns with dark memories and fears. Mary, too, remains sober and pretends to listen intently to Bill and Bob. It is a relief for both of them when the speeches start.

After the speeches, dancing commences, but Beverly asks Bill to take her home because she has a headache. In the car, Bill asks, "Are you feeling alright?"

"Sure. I'm just tired."

Bill doesn't push any further, but the silence is deafening. After making sure Beverly is comfortable on the couch with some good tea and a pain reliever, Bill does not linger long before he heads home for the night.

Beverly finishes the tea and heads off to bed where she spends hours thumbing through old magazines, unable to muster the courage to turn out the light. Thoughts run randomly through her head.

With all of her faults, Mary does not seem like a murderess, but what about Bob? Did Bob and Mary conspire to get rid of Ellen? Was Mary's little white lie about her jewelry just a coincidence?

All through the weekend, Beverly goes through the motions of being the mom, doing housework, food shopping, going to church and making small talk with her kids. Bill comes over on Sunday afternoon.

To him, Beverly seems curiously cold. Out of guilt, she makes him and the kids a nice supper of pork chops, mashed potatoes, and corn – comfort foods. Bill and the kids enjoy the meal, which partially makes up for Beverly's demeanor.

Chapter 16: Reluctant Monday

On Monday morning, Beverly wakes up about ten minutes before the alarm goes off from a restless sleep. The morning silence speaks of impending danger. After waking the kids, she dallies in the shower, but at the last possible minute she is dutifully making sure the kids are off to school, not bothering to banter with them and surprising each with a hug as they go out the door.

Slow traffic transfixes the world as thoughts wind through the corridors of her mind. Perhaps she should call Detective Simmons, but what would she tell her? Detectives probably get all kinds of calls from crackpots who think that they have unraveled a mystery.

Not everything reaches the news media – perhaps the murders at *Gerry's Socks & Shoes* have already been solved. Wouldn't THAT be embarrassing? Anyway, Anna's death, supposedly, was a suicide.

Tears burn Beverly's face as she remembers Ellen's open eyes, Anna demanding to know why Beverly was at her desk and Mary's incongruence in her apparent lies. What evil lurks at *Gerry's Socks & Shoes*? What would happen to her kids if Beverly was murdered today? Would their dad suddenly become responsible? Would Bill wonder if she loved him?

Beverly arrives at work earlier than usual, allowing her to take a front parking space. Her shoes click in double time as she scurries up the stairway to her cubicle and valiantly fights her fears.

At her desk she searches for Detective Simmons' phone number among the large pile of sticky notes and business cards. Finding it, she tucks it securely under her keyboard for safekeeping. Her instincts will tell her when the time is right to call.

At eleven thirty, Beverly is in a boardroom with nine other people (including Mary) discussing a new ad campaign, feeling her morning coffee. When the meeting breaks, she takes the "safety in numbers" rule and follows the rest of the attendees to the restroom.

Seeing that Mary is following her, she rushes to finish her business to avoid conversation. Heart beating wildly, she is out of breath when she gets back to her desk, grabs her purse and heads out for lunch.

"Are you going to lunch?" Mary asks casually as she passes Beverly in the hall.

"No, I've got errands to run." Beverly lies.

"Oh . . . would you like some company?"

"No . . . not today. I just want to hurry up and get done. Have a good lunch, though, OK?"

"You, too!" Mary replies, actually sounding sincere and extremely unstressed, leaving Beverly wondering if her jealously of Mary's youth and finesse have tricked her imagination.

By the end of the day, Beverly realizes that Monday has been totally uneventful.

* * * * *

Tuesday morning there are police cars outside *Gerry's Socks & Shoes* as Beverly drives into the parking lot. She exits her car and surveys the building. Pane glass windows reveal security guards chatting with police officers inside. Other employees are walking into the building, eyes wide-open like children in an amusement park.

Numbly, Beverly enters the building. After scanning her employee badge, she heads directly up the stairs. There, the entire workforce is standing out in the hallway, some with their morning coffee in hand, noisily discussing what is going on. There is an officer at the desk where Anna used to sit, doing some kind of search. All entryways to get into the cubicle area where employees sit are taped off with yellow tape. The mood of the employees seems jovial, probably because what is happening is more exciting than reading email.

"What is going on?" Beverly asks the group closest to the stairway.

"They are not saying, but they have found surveillance cameras in the building that I don't believe belong to security. We can't go back to our desks until the search is over," responds Ted, a junior accountant in the finance department who speaks in a high-pitched tone for a man. He is short in stature with baby blue eyes and a wayward frock of greasy, blonde hair skimming over his pimple-ridden forehead.

"Do you mean that someone has been spying on us?" Beverly asks with concern. Did someone see her find the gun in Anna's cube?

"Probably a competitor or something," Ted responds with a nervous laugh. Conversation turns to the many examples everyone has hearsay of spying on various companies, as well as the cameras and equipment used to do it. As each speaker tops the previous speaker, the hallway becomes increasingly noisier and the clock ticks past eight thirty. Finally, the HR Director tells all employees to go home for the day and like kids on a holiday, they are all more than pleased to oblige.

Upon arriving home, Beverly calls Bill at work. "You are not going to believe this," she begins.

"The butler did it with a hammer in the drawing room?" Bill answers, obviously not quite in synch with Beverly's feelings.

"We were all sent home today because they found an unauthorized surveillance system on our floor."

"You're kidding, right? You must work in the most crisis-oriented company I have ever heard of!"

"I'm not kidding."

"Well, enjoy your day off! You seemed kind of distant all weekend. Have you been feeling OK?"

"Yes. I have just had a lot on my mind." Guilt twinges in Beverly's gut.

"You know that I'm always here for you, right?"

"Yes and I don't deserve it." She should have stopped the conversation there, but she finds herself saying, "I don't know if I ever really admitted this to you, Bill, but I do love you."

The pause is long. "I love you, too, Beverly. I'll come by tonight, OK?"

"OK."

Hanging up the phone, Beverly finds herself in tears. *'What a bitch I am! Bill is my prince in shining armor; confidant; best and only true friend. What would I do without him? Perhaps it is time to give him my body and soul . . . I wonder what he would be like in bed . . .'*

After allowing herself to carry on for some time, she slowly begins to straighten her house. Deep down she knows that she will never sleep with Bill until she is sure he is the "one", they are engaged (committed), the kids are on their way to success, and . . .

Chapter 17: Company Announcement

Any level of comfort Beverly has at her desk this morning disintegrates when Lana, Senior Vice President, quicksteps to her desk to tell her to be in the main conference room in ten minutes. The rumor mill has painted Lana as a tyrant with few feelings and behind her back they taunt "all ways are the Queen's ways." With timeless beauty and a flair for suits, she lets you know immediately that she is in control.

Lana's urgency makes Beverly sure that she is some kind of trouble. Her hands shake as she looks through her email, where she finally finds the meeting notice to all managers, senior managers and directors on Beverly's floor at 8:30 a.m. What a relief to know she will not be facing Lana alone.

By the time Beverly reaches the conference room, it is buzzing with gossip. It is obvious that everyone is antsy for the meeting to begin. Many people are talking about yesterday's security breech discoveries. When the CEO approaches the podium at the head of the room everyone quiets down. There is no doubt this is serious business.

"As some of you already know, there has been a security breech in our building. Two remote surveillance cameras were found on the second floor, as well as two remote transceivers. What we have not found is the computer or other device that was being used as the receiver. As you can imagine, this has made us very insecure about the confidentiality of proprietary information."

For the next thirty minutes, the CEO proceeds with a speech about security and confidentiality and how managers need to work with their teams to protect it; what to watch out for; and procedures for reporting anything suspicious. There are slides changing behind him to emphasize his speech, but most of the time he is blocking them with his shadow.

When the handsome, grey-haired CEO finally takes a breath and asks for questions, many hands go up and everyone in the room spends the next half hour listening to people's concerns and questions. No, management does not know how long these cameras have been in place. The cameras are not very expensive and could have been bought and set up by an amateur.

After the meeting, Beverly thinks to herself that Bill was right; *Gerry's Socks & Shoes* seems to be experiencing abnormal situations. Unfortunately, her next meeting does not add any confidence in the company's situation. She learns that the company's quarterly sales are down and the managers in attendance seem completely out of new ideas (or perhaps distracted by their previous meeting).

The Shoes Product Manager wines that she needs the sock campaign complete by Monday for a combined ad that Beverly understood was not supposed to be released until next month. Everyone leaves the meeting sober and overwhelmed.

When Beverly calls the her kids to tell them she will be late, they do not seem upset and Bill just repeats what he always says to her, that she needs rest. At 5:30 pm, the majority of her co-workers are gone. Several people linger on in the office for the next half hour, but by 6:00, the silence speaks of complete solitude.

Beverly tries to stay focused, but she finds her mind wondering off to Mary's lie, Ellen's murder and Anna's supposed suicide. Her fears aggravate the silence. To ease stress, she stands up and takes a short walk.

The floor resonates silent and empty. The only sound is the buzz of the halogen lights. When she returns to her desk, she is disturbed by the sound of a door closing and footsteps. She jumps out of her chair to see Bob coming from his office with his briefcase, looking very tired and disheveled.

"Oh! Hi, Bob!" Beverly half-yells to get his attention, trying to show a natural grin, "I thought I was the only one here."

As Bob approaches, she cannot help but feel sympathy for him. He, honestly, does not look good. "No, I had a lot of work to catch up on. How are you, Beverly?"

"Fine. And you?"

"Just a little stressed. It's actually hard for me to work late these days. I should be home with the kids."

"I know the feeling." Beverly replies soberly. Bob's face looks extremely sad. "Once you and Mary are married things should be easier."

"Yeah. I guess so. She isn't warming up to the kids like I thought she would, though. I thought that because she had her own child, she would learn to love mine."

"Some things only come with time."

"I know."

"There is another thing, though . . ." Bob begins, but then he looks like he has changed his mind about what he was going to say.

"What's that?" prods Beverly.

"This may just seem stupid, but the other day I found Mary trying on Ellen's jewelry that I had stashed away in the closet. Ellen had some very valuable pieces and I wanted my daughter to have them someday."

"Well, she may have felt that you wouldn't mind now that you are engaged."

"Maybe, but later, when I put them away in a better place, I noticed that there are pieces missing. Mary says the kids probably got into them and that she found the box dumped on the bedroom floor. I suppose that could have happened, but I don't know . . ."

"Kids do tend to get into things." Beverly offers.

"Yes. I know, but I just found out that Lisa, my assistant, was out of the office when Ellen called the day that she was killed. I'm sure it is just a coincidence, but Ellen called Mary to check my schedule and Mary says she forgot to leave me the message. It probably would not have changed what happened, but I would have been watching for Ellen if I had known she was coming." He starts to lose his composure. "I've got to go get my kids," he says, turning to leave.

The fear of staying in that building alone bolts Beverly out of her chair, "Wait a minute, Bob, would you walk out with me?"

"Sure."

She gets her things and they leave together. The silence is uncomfortable, so Beverly again tries to say the right thing, "Kids do all kinds of crazy things. My kids lost my keys one year and I found them two years later under the bathroom sink in a jar."

"Yeah. Stuff happens, I suppose."

"How do you know that Ellen called Mary?"

"Lisa told me that Ellen called her when she got back to her desk to tell her that she was running late. Lisa said she would check my schedule to make sure I was available, but Ellen told her that Mary had already taken care of that."

"Was your schedule free for that time?"

"Yeah. I'm sure that it just slipped Mary's mind to tell me that Ellen called. I decided to run errands, so I was not there when Ellen came."

As Beverly fights the traffic home, she tries to piece together what she knows about Mary. Her thoughts will not leave her alone. Finally at home, she scans through her DVD's for a fairytale to take her away to an enchanted journey far from thoughts of murder and espionage, but nothing appeals to her. The piano in the corner calls her to play something, but nothing she can play matches the emotion she must expel.

When the children are finally off to bed and she is alone at the kitchen table, she goes to her computer to work on her book that she had put aside after the murder. But as has been the case ever since she began writing, the story completely changes. How surprised she is when a revised morbid version pours out like a fierce wind.

The clouded skies are dark at an hour when most people sleep as rain sheets down on cobblestone streets drizzled with reflected streaks of light. Children cry and mothers quietly weep as they line up behind weathered trucks under the supervision of men and boys with sober faces in military uniforms. Low voices and flashlights direct the weary and distraught family groups to their travel places on wet, wooden floors of open-bed trucks.

A twelve-year-old girl, slightly budding with puberty, is dressed in her best white dress with a dowdy coat thrown over and a bright blue, beaded ornament in her long hair. As she gets ready to load into the truck with her mother and infant brother, the handsome young soldier organizing the load asks her to load into the next truck in the convoy.

Although her mother protests, her stoic father standing by to say goodbye, reassures her that the child will be fine. He takes the young girl's hand into his and rubs it softly with his thumb until the time comes to load her into the next truck. After giving her instructions to join her mother at their destination, he softly kisses her goodbye. Tears line his eyes as he waves and then dutifully heads back to his regiment. The little girl remains brave for her father, knowing the situation is dire, but she cannot contain the tears that have now worn dirty streams down her face.

As the soldiers leave to load the next truck, the little girl panics as she remembers that she left the water bottle she was responsible for on a bench at the side of a nearby building. She calls one of the soldiers and asks if she can go to get the water and he offers to take her.

Lifting her down, he accidentally pulls the front of her dress down, slightly revealing her small breasts. He takes her hand and leads her off, but he does not take her to the bench. When she starts to protest, he tells her that they need to do something else first.

Through the rain they trudge down an empty street. He opens the door to one of the evacuated houses and takes the girl in. As he searches the house with his gun aimed forward, the girl waits impatiently, knowing that she must get back to the truck before the convoy leaves.

"You sure are a pretty little girl," the man says, coming out of the kitchen with a stolen beer. The little girl feels uncomfortable with how he looks at her.

"I need to get my water and get back to the truck," she says, biting her lip. The man pulls on the top of her dress and reveals her breasts on purpose.

The young girl stands shocked and totally speechless. He then reaches for her and gives her a hug. She stiffens. Without a word, he begins undressing her and touching her genitals and she begins to fight furiously, feeling the warmth of sexuality in her groin and guilt for feeling it. Her scream is weak and he spanks her hard for letting it out. No one hears.

"Don't fight me," he whispers in her ear, "you know that you want it."

In silence, she allows him to violate her body as she suffers with small whimpers—mortified that someone might walk in and find her with him. She only opens her eyes in brief interludes, horrified at the appearance of the grown man's body in its aroused state. Never did she imagine that the romantic acts she had imagined from her small knowledge of sex would be so painful, messy and smelly.

After the sexual act is done, the man continues to fondle her for what seems like forever. When she finally risks opening her eyes, she sees him looking at her with regret.

"Go to sleep, little Girl. Just go to sleep," he tells her as she lays there for what seems like hours, waiting for him to leave her alone.

When he finally dozes off, the little girl tries to rationalize what has happened. She peeks out at him and surmises that he looks like a kind man. He must have been so taken with her beauty that he could not help himself. Perhaps in this time of war, there was not time to wait for her to grow up and love to take its course. Finally, with the comforting thought that what happened was out of admiration for her and eternal love, she settles into his arms and falls asleep.

When the girl awakes, she is alone and there is an eerie silence in the house. In the far distance, she can hear guns and explosions. In fear, she gets up and runs for the front door, but horror sets in as she observes the man she had shared intimacy with just a few short hours ago on the couch, looking very dead, with his hands and wrists cut and blood pooling onto the carpet below. Taking in a large breath of horror, she musters all of the courage she has to bypass him, open the door, and set herself free onto the village street that now seems very strange, dark and empty.

The rain has stopped, but the steady stream of tears burn her face. Terrified, in pain, violated and ashamed, she makes her way through the streets like a little mouse hiding from predators, until she finally finds a house with the door unlocked and goes inside. A clock in the kitchen says it is 3:00 a.m. Stealing bedcovers, she makes herself a place to sleep under the bed and prays for forgiveness and world peace unceasingly until exhaustion relieves her once more with sleep.

After a few short hours of restless sleep, she awakes to the sound of guns. For nearly an hour the young heart imagines her father, brothers, uncles, friends, and clergy being killed as she adheres to her hiding place. The tears turn to anger and make her feel brave as she finally ventures out from the safety of her hiding place. She prays frantically and confidently as she runs out of the house, down the street and straight into the streets where gunshots ring out randomly from both sides.

"Stop!" she pleads, but no one hears her over the din. Like a moving target in a video game, she is immediately shot down and falls like a limp doll.

Only four men witness the girl's murder and two are her killers. The other two recognize her as a local child, which fuels their rage, giving them strength far beyond their own capabilities to initiate a cyclone of rage. Like savage beasts they kill until they are brought down and buried among the growing debris of corpses. As each warrior is cut down, two others feed on their rage, causing men and woman to do things that those of us who were not there feel we would never do, severing limbs and mutilating bodies without remorse. Eventually, the girl's body is completely buried and forgotten.

Imaginative stories will forever color history books with theories about why the village was victorious. Not even the survivors would believe that the death of one small girl escalated the anger enough to be the primary contributor to the battle outcome. Her disappearance will haunt her family for years. They will never know that in one day she grew up and changed the destiny of their world.

The wadded-up tissue in Beverly's hand only burns her tear-stained face and leaves residual lint on her face. What in the world has compelled her to write with such disregard for morality and the pursuit of justice?

Perhaps her own life events leave her feeling violated with evil flanking her on each side, mimicking and mocking her while her prayers and pleadings seem unheeded by God. *What would you have me say or do, Dear God, to win your favor? Why have you abandoned me?*

Beverly has to face the hard truth that the rage in this story is her own. Who killed Ellen? Why did Anna die? Why is God so silent? Is the sexuality in the story a product of her deprivation or of the feelings she has towards an ex-husband who had the gall to deflower her and then leave her like a whore?

Is it her intuition or imagination that intertwines the security breech at *Gerry's Socks & Shoes* with Ellen's murder and Anna's death? Where does Mary fit in the picture or is she just a victim of circumstances? Do thoughts rule your dreams or do dreams have a life of their own with no rhyme or reason?

Slowly a new scenario weaves in Beverly's mind. Suppose the person or persons monitoring the remote cameras saw Ellen enter the restroom, followed her in and put the yellow "Restroom Closed" sandwich boards outside to make people believe the restroom was being cleaned. After they killed her, they removed the sandwich boards and left. Perhaps Anna saw the murderer exit the restroom.

Beverly stands up to wake herself from madness and take a deep breath. She deduces that an office building does not seem the most fruitful target for a good heist, especially not the bathroom, so why would the women's rings be missing? Closing her eyes, she tries to reconstruct Ellen's murder scene and again recalls the purse on the floor next to the toilet that was not taken.

Both women had very expensive rings. Beverly recalls that Jennifer said that Anna actually had an eternity ring with many large diamonds across the front. How would the murderer know the rings were valuable? The thief had to know the victims!

Again, Beverly focuses on the Mary factor. Aside from the fact that Mary's vanity is annoying and she is not the quintessence of trustworthiness, Beverly does not see her as intelligent enough to be the murderess. She is obsessed with external things, such as hair, nails and clothes and openly vies for the attention of wealthy men because she abhors being alone.

Before Bob's wife died, Mary was overtly flirtatious with him. Did she aspire to be his wife? Could Mary be devious and heartless enough to kill a wife and mother for her own benefit?

Beverly sits down and mulls her questions. She will not sleep much tonight. In fact, since finding Ellen, Beverly has not slept well for months and she knows that sleep deprivation is starting the affect her work and her inward thoughts.

She buries her manuscript in a series of folders on her computer memory stick to make it difficult for anyone else to find. She feels ashamed of how morbid and sexually explicit her writing has become, but does not want to destroy the power of the emotions she feels in this rendition of the story. Not fully understanding how the writing and her feelings meld together, she does know they are somehow intertwined.

Chapter 18: Covert Affairs

This morning Beverly is on her own undercover mission. "Good morning, Mary! Do you still have Jennifer's new work number?"

Mary looks a little startled. On her computer screen is a Web site that Beverly has seen her watching before, where she can tune into her son's preschool classroom to view what he is doing. It is a perk many childcare facilities offer to assure parents that their programs are safe. "Uh . . . Good morning! Sure. Let me get it."

"Which one is your son?"

Mary smiles and looks a little relieved that Beverly does not seem judgmental. "There he is," she points out on the screen. She then starts fishing around in her sticky notes and pulls out one. "And here is your number!"

"Ivan is so cute . . ." Beverly confesses, realizing it really is hard to see Mary as a murderess. "Well, I'd better get back to work. Bye!" Beverly heads back to her desk.

On Jennifer's voice mail, Beverly leaves a message: "Hello, Jennifer. This is Beverly Scott. I've been meaning to call for quite a while to catch up with you, but just recently got your number from Mary. Would you like to meet for lunch today? My number here is 339-2222. Call me when you get a chance!"

The morning seems unusually long as Beverly waits for Jennifer to respond. Finally, at eleven-thirty Jennifer calls and seems genuinely pleased to hear from Beverly. Of course, she doesn't know she is going to be interrogated. They make lunch plans for noon, which means Beverly must leave in fifteen minutes, but procrastination makes her sift through her email a little too long and she arrives at the restaurant a little late.

"Beverly!" Jennifer calls, waiving from her table.

"Hello! How are you! You look great!" She really does with her once long hair cut into a chin-length, business-looking coif and sporting a bright yellow suit coat with black trim, black blouse and pants.

"Oh, I am! You look great, yourself!" she answers.

They read the menu as they catch up on each other. Jennifer is finishing her Bachelor's degree at night school and has been promoted to office manager. Beverly finds herself feeling a bit jealous, because her own career is relatively unchanged.

Once their meals are served, Beverly opens up the subject that they have both been avoiding. "Jennifer, have you thought of anything Anna said before she died that may have given you a hint that she knew something about Ellen's murder?"

Jennifer's facial expression changes and she holds her fork in mid-air, looking up as if she needs to catch her thoughts. "I think about it sometimes, but I'm not really sure if she knew anything. Why?"

"They found cameras and transceivers in our building last week. Someone had been monitoring our hallways upstairs. If those monitors have been there awhile, then someone could have seen Ellen go into the restroom. If Anna witnessed something, maybe she was caught on camera, too."

"Weird, but Ellen's murder was so long ago. Do you really think the cameras were there that long?"

"Perhaps I'm just grasping at straws, but I am still haunted by memories of finding Ellen's body. I just wish the whole thing was resolved so I could stop thinking about it."

"I know. I think that Anna and I could have been great friends if she would not have died. We had a lot in common."

"But, you don't remember anything that she told you that could be a clue to what happened?"

"Well . . . maybe. You are going to think I'm a nut case, though!"

"I doubt it!" Beverly coaches her with a slight smile. "Why?"

"Anna told me that Mary was having an affair another woman."

"That's nuts." Beverly says with surety.

"I would have thought so, too, but about a month before the murders, Mary asked me to go to a club with her. When I got there, she introduced me to another woman named Nancy. They both got drunk and started talking derogatory about men, saying they only made good 'sugar daddies.' When I decided to leave (because it was getting too ridiculous for me to stay), Mary tried to keep me there and then she gave me a hug that made me feel very uncomfortable and I left."

"You left by yourself?"

"Yes. I was never comfortable with Mary again, even though we had been friends for years. But that's not all. When I met Nancy, I thought I had seen her somewhere before. The next day at work, I saw her cleaning the hallway. She is one of people on the cleaning team in your building."

"Really? I really can't see Mary dating a janitor – especially a woman janitor! I wonder what the draw would be." Beverly still is not convinced.

"Well, they both seemed pretty mad at men that night."

"If Mary measures a man by the diamonds he presents, I just don't get why she would be involved with a female janitor." Beverly replies.

"Yes, but you know what she does with all the jewelry she is given after a break-up, don't you?"

"No . . ."

"I don't know how she does it, but men seem compelled to buy Mary expensive jewelry. She has shown me pieces that must be worth thousands of dollars! When she breaks up with someone, she keeps the jewelry and often has the stones re-set into new pieces. She has had all kinds of valuable pieces made from ex-wedding and engagement rings, as well as other gorgeous pieces that she has received!"

"Oh my gosh! I have never heard that."

"She used to brag to me about it all the time."

Beverly takes a small bite of her lunch as she digests what she has heard. "Jennifer, you are not going to believe this, but Bob told me that he was missing some of Ellen's jewelry and that possibly Mary took it. At the time I didn't think that would happen, but now I wonder."

"I don't really think Mary would steal. Did Bob and Mary break up?"

"Not yet, I don't believe, but Bob seemed disenchanted with her last time I talked to him."

"Guess I didn't know that you ever talked to Bob. If that is true, though, it's unfortunate. In our last phone call, Mary sounded like she really loves him."

"Really? So, do you think that she is bi-sexual?"

"Oh my gosh, no! Mary just likes to have fun!"

"Well, I always wondered why you weren't having lunch with Mary as much anymore. You guys used to eat together every day."

After lunch, Beverly tries to process the new information, but it all seems too bazaar to be true. By midafternoon she is trying to concentrate on her ad campaign when her phone rings.

"Hi, Beverly. This is Mary. Did you get a hold of Jennifer?"

"Yes! We had lunch together."

"Oh! You should have invited me! I haven't seen her in so long. How was she?" Mary oozes.

"She seemed to be doing very well."

"I miss her – especially when I'm having a day like today . . ."

"I'm sorry you're having a bad day. What's going on?" Beverly baby-talks her.

Mary's voice lowers her voice as she says, "I can't talk here. What are you doing after work?"

Fear flip-flops in Beverly's gut, but she answers, "I can stay a few minutes. Do you want to just meet in your cubical after work?"

"Sure – or – if Bob leaves early, we can use his office."

Sheer horror has invaded Beverly's imagination and meeting alone with Mary does not seem like a good idea. The mixture of what she has seen and heard has stirred her reality so thoroughly that she can no longer distinguish imaginable fabrications from concrete facts. Is this a panic attack?

As she hangs up the phone, she has a feeling that time is suspended and her career that once seemed her livelihood now seems totally irrelevant to life. Could sweet, little blonde Mary, who is totally incapable of being alone and seems to have few, if any of her own ideas, have anything to do with murder?

That evening, Tania calls Beverly to report that she and the boys are home from school. Beverly tries to hold her on the phone, but Tania shortens the call, saying she has to call her boyfriend. Beverly toys with the idea to call her mother for reassurance, but knows that her silent screams would never be heard above her mother's impractical advice and glowing details about her sister's kids. If she told Bill, he would surely believe that she needed serious psychological counseling and that would probably scare him away.

Her thoughts magnify her isolation as she quietly observes time accelerating towards closing time with no way to stop it. At 5:00 p.m., coworkers rapidly begin to thin out as Beverly waits silently in her chair, pretending to scan emails. By 5:15, the office is nearly silent and she slowly begins her journey to Mary's cubicle.

"Oh! You're here! Bob's office is empty, so let's go in there," Mary encourages.

Bob's office is painted a stately federal blue with light gray woodwork. Dark wood bookcases line the wall on Beverly's left and a tall window with stainless steel blinds covers most of the middle wall.

The broad, square legs of the massive desk are etched with bold, vertical lines and the top is slate-black, elegantly framed in matching wood. To Beverly's right is a variety of artwork, including a large image of the New York skyline that she finds an odd choice for an office in Seattle.

To get the ball rolling (so she can get home), Beverly begins, "You seemed a bit upset this afternoon. What's going on?"

"Bob and I had a fight and I was in the wrong," Mary says sadly.

"Did you tell him that?"

"No. It was so stupid! Bob had a box of Ellen's jewelry in his closet. I spent the night with him and did some of his laundry. Actually, I spent several nights with him, but anyway, I found the jewelry."

"That doesn't seem like it would start a fight . . ."

"When he got home, he caught me trying it on. He was so angry that I quickly dumped it all back in the box, but later he said some was missing."

Beverly pretends she has not heard the story before. "Do you think one of the kids got into it?"

Mary starts to cry. "Actually, before he got there, I had put some in my pocket. I figured it would be mine after we married, anyway, but he told me after he found it missing that he wanted his kids to have it when they grow up. I should have guessed that and I had no business putting any in my pocket. Now, I don't know how to tell him that I took it and give it back."

Both tongues fall silent for a short time and Mary grabs a tissue to wipe her face and blow her nose. Her puppy-dog eyes sucker Beverly into contemplating what can be done. "Mary, why don't you just tell him the truth?"

In tears, Mary answers helplessly, "How would you feel if you found out your fiancé took some of your dead wife's jewelry? I just don't know how to tell him! I don't even know what made me think it was mine."

"Where is it now?"

"I have it at home."

"Are you guys still seeing each other?"

"We still spend time together, but he is distant. I pray and pray that God will change his heart, but I don't think God hears me! I am so scared that I will lose him!" Now she is sobbing.

Beverly's supercilious beliefs are that Mary would only think about God if she wanted something. Mary makes up her own rules and hopes that God will accept her excuses at the Golden Gate.

On the other hand, Mary does seem remorseful for what she did. In the years Beverly has worked with her, she has never known her to be mean or spiteful to anyone. She recalls the time that Mary brought her flowers and took her out to lunch for her birthday, because the rest of the office had forgotten.

"Perhaps," Beverly realizes to herself, *"I am the one being uncharitable."* Then she recalls these lines attributed to Jesus in the New Testament: *"You hypocrite! First take the log out of your own eye, and then you will see clearly to take the speck out of your brother's eye."* Of course, in this case it would be her sister's eye . . .

Bowing her head and asking God for forgiveness, Beverly offers a plan that includes a little white lie. "Mary, maybe you should just put the jewelry back in the house somewhere where Bob will find it. He will probably believe that the kids got into it and the incident will be water under the bridge."

How in the world could this beautiful blonde, devastated by her own guilt for such a small misunderstanding, be a murderer or a thief? Is there not an inkling of a fairy tale that can stand up to real life? Send in the clowns . . .

Chapter 19: Not all Hidden is Fabricated

Beverly's eyes feel heavy and hollow from many nights of little sleep that have corrupted her reality with a touch of insanity. The radio alarm annoys her with petty, emotional songs that she no longer finds relevant. Turning it off, she forces herself to get up, promising herself that she will change it to an alarm tone for tomorrow morning. Then she reaches for the tablet on the side of her bed where she had written a poem to Bill before her discourse with Mary:

> *Sing to me,*
> *Sing to me,*
> *Tell me your dream,*
> *Tell me your laughter, your sorrow, your grief.*
> *Tell the sweet maple to send me a leaf*
> *To wear in my hair*
> *When the sun comes to stay.*

The love and romance she portrayed in those lines seemed so profound and true when she scribed them, but this morning they seem hollow. She contemplates if thoughts of Bill conjure feelings of love, sexual desire, or only the comfort that she "has someone."

Tears fall without restraint as she mulls the haunting darkness in her heart. Did her X-husband ever really love her? Does anyone really ever love anyone or do we collect people like possessions? If love exists, is she loveable? After years of being in love, are you still beautiful to your lover or just familiar like an old couch?

If someone murdered her today, would the universe feel even the slightest ripple? Is it reality or insanity that makes her whole being tense like a doe sensing peril? Should she tell her mother, Bill, the kids or the detective about the insane fears that paralyze her? How much of what she feels is real and how much does her imagination fabricate? *'When I am gone, will I be remembered or will memories of me be absorbed into insignificant pollutants? Does even God love me? I can't BELIEVE I told Mary to lie.'*

Habit enables Beverly to rouse her children and get them off to school. She arrives at work on time, but the whole day is a blur. By 5:00 p.m., she is overwhelmed by email, layouts to complete, and a quarterly budget due yesterday.

The clock says 5:20 before she notices that the building has grown very quiet. Irrational fear picks at her like a devil prodding her with a stick. Realizing that she needs to use the restroom only aggravates her fear. To keep her bearings, she works harder and faster so that she can get to a stopping place and leave, but her sore bladder is distracting.

Suddenly, her hearing seems enhanced as she picks up a quiet conversation on the stairs. She stands up in her cubicle to see the cleaning team, two women that she sees every day. The older woman, probably in her fifties, is sturdy with long, brown hair pulled back and streaked with gray. The other woman is young and tall, with not much of a bust and short, curly red hair. Beverly suspects that the younger one is Nancy. When they look up, she realizes that she is intruding and guiltily returns to her chair.

She tries to continue working, but like a wild animal her senses reach out for sights, smells, and sounds of danger. Beverly's heart thumps wildly until she hears the women head down the stairs. Exasperated with her imagination, she packs up to leave. Obviously, she cannot work tonight. If evil were personified, it would be lurking in *Gerry's Socks & Shoes* at night in full black garb, yellow cat eyes staring at all those who cannot leave well-enough alone until tomorrow.

Soon she is walking out the front door, where the parking lot appears to be deserted. There is a sidewalk with landscaping on one side (trees and shrubs) that goes all the way to the back of the parking lot where Beverly is parked. As she heads towards her car, she suddenly hears a rustle in the bushes behind her and then footsteps.

She contemplates whether she should turn around, but before she makes up her mind, she feels an arm around her neck and another across her chest. Her mouth opens to scream as a cloth covers her nose and mouth. She smells a familiar medicinal aroma and falls into a very strange state where she can hear women talking and feel someone pulling her around, but she cannot stop them.

Using all the concentration she can muster, she tries to force her eyes open, but has little control over her head or limbs. She sees only the ground. The last thing she hears is a scream and like she is watching a broken movie reel, Beverly's mind flickers and goes blank.

Her next memory is of someone trying to put something up her nose, but she cannot find enough strength to fight. Slowly she tries to make sense out of the sights and sounds and realizes that she is in an ambulance. A man in green scrubs is trying to calm her.

As the clouds of comatose thin out, Beverly acknowledges an ambulance ride, doctor and nurse examinations, and then questioning, questioning, and more questioning. Apparently, the suspects got away and her sparse memories – again! – do not seem to help the police. The only clear memory she has is that scream . . .

Chapter 20: After Shocks

"Did you know that Mary is in a coma?" Bob asks Beverly, who is sitting on the side of the bed with her table tray in front of her while Bill sits in the hospital recliner. Bob surprised her when he came to visit, flowers in hand. Bill had welcomed him warmly, probably feeling lucky to have male company. Up until this question, they had all been just talking to be polite about nearly nothing. The overhead TV is on, but the volume is so low that no one can really hear it.

"No. I didn't hear that. What happened?" Beverly asks in shock.

"The detectives were hoping you would know, but I guess you were pretty out of it. Mary was working late and was beat up pretty bad the same night you were attacked. Her injuries are mostly head and back injuries and she has not regained consciousness. She was found on a road about two blocks from *Gerry's Socks & Shoes*." Bob looks like he is going to cry.

"Didn't Security see anything on the cameras?"

"No. Months after Ellen was murdered," Bob's voice is breaking, "management finally bought cameras to monitor the upstairs, which is how they found the unauthorized system strung out up there. Before Ellen's murder, all of the cameras were at the entrances and exits of the building. There have never been cameras in the parking lot." Bob looks down.

"Are you OK, Bob?" Beverly asks.

"I just don't want to lose Mary. I keep thinking there must have been something I could do . . . "

"Don't beat yourself up, Bob." Bill says in a trite male attempt at consolation.

Beverly's thoughts go internal. *What if she never comes back? Who will care for her little son? I thought everyone was out of the building that night, but was Mary still there? What happened to the cleaning women? Was it Mary who screamed?'* Beverly says a little prayer for Bob, Mary, and Mary's son, as Bill tries to console Bob.

After the two men leave, Beverly tries to reconstruct what she remembers, but Mary is not in the picture at all. As far as she knew, only she and the two cleaning ladies were in the building. Even the guard at the door was gone for the day.

Chapter 21: Confronting Mary

The hospital seemed so safe and sterile, like an enormous brick castle with many merry maids taking care of all Beverly's needs, but home leaves her overwhelmed with housework and too much time to think. The doctor's orders were sedatives, two weeks off work, and the psychological counseling that up to now she had been able to avoid, hiding the depth of her insanity.

The kids were thoughtful and brought her flowers when she was in the hospital. Bill helped them clean up the house before she came home. Now they act like nothing has happened and bicker and complain constantly. Beverly's numb disposition irritates and aggravates their behavior as they vie for attention she is not capable of providing.

Her mother insists that she should quit her job, but Beverly does not see that as an option without another job in place. The many resumes she has sent out to escape this nightmare seem to have vanished into the wind.

She has never prayed so hard for a life change. *'God, are you there? While Noah tended his glorious petting barn, was he glad to be alive or were his dreams filled with morbid thoughts of millions of people drowning, buried under the sea with children in their arms? Would a new job in a new place only mask the ghosts lingering in the tide for me? Is the only way to save myself from insanity to dive under the dark waters and face my most horrendous fears? Oh God! Help me!'*

The solitude while her kids are at school allows Beverly to flash back, trying to reconstruct what she could see and hear from that frightful night. She wishes that she had forced her eyes open earlier, before the sedative had taken so much effect. No matter how hard she tries, she cannot identify the assailants, but she does vaguely remember they were both women.

She has foggy visions of two figures, but cannot separate memories from bad dreams and imagination. She wishes particularly that she could place those tired brown eyes that haunt her, as well as the voice that did the heavy whispering in breathless, short statements like,

"Put her down." Then, there was a haunting memory of a scream that now she believes could have been Mary's. Poor Mary.

Three days ago, Bob called Beverly from the hospital to tell her that Mary had awakened from her coma. Beverly longs to talk to her, but the hospital phone in Mary's room has been continually busy, which hints that Mary's setback has not changed her social life.

The phone startles Beverly's thoughts. She feels like she is awaking from a very bad dream. "Hello," she answers soberly.

"Hi, Beverly. This is Mary." a familiar little voice responds in baby-talk without its usual lift.

"Mary! Are you OK? Are you out of the hospital?"

"Yes, but we need to talk and I can't talk here. Will you meet me somewhere?"

Beverly feels a panic attack coming just thinking about leaving the house alone. She knows it is irrational, so she bravely responds, "Where do you want to meet?"

"How about at that little Chinese place on First Street for lunch at noon?"

"Yes . . . but, Mary . . ."

"I can't talk right now. I'll see you this afternoon at eleven-thirty, OK?"

Patience is not one of Beverly's virtues as she sits in the restaurant. Scoping the doorway, she finally sees a shape that resembles Mary, sunglasses hiding her eyes and visible bruises on her face and arms.

"Hi," Mary says timidly, dropping her purse on the table and taking a seat.

"Hi."

"Don't look at me that way. I know I look terrible," she says bowing her head. Looking around nervously, she surprises Beverly with a direct question, "Do you have a suspect?"

"No."

Mary's frown deepens. "It was Nancy."

"Nancy, the cleaning lady? Did you tell the police?"

"No. I was hoping you would have something to support my theory. Do you mind telling me what you think happened?"

"I don't know . . . I was working late. I heard the cleaning women come up the stairs with their equipment, but in just a few minutes it seemed like they disappeared and the silence spooked me, so I packed up my stuff and left. In the parking lot, two woman grabbed me from the back. I don't remember much else."

"Was one of the cleaning woman you saw tall with short, curly red hair?"

"Yes."

"Her name is Nancy."

"I didn't know that."

"Then, why did you say 'Nancy, the cleaning lady'?"

"I've never met either of them."

"The older woman's name is Cindy."

Beverly is confused and cannot imagine Mary having an affair with an older woman. "Why do you think Nancy would come after me?"

"I don't know."

The silent contemplation engulfs them for several seconds before the waitress comes to take their order. Neither of them has looked at the menu, but they both order sesame chicken with hot tea.

Mary's mouth is drawn tight. Her face appears raw and sore.

"Mary, how do you know Nancy?" Beverly continues the conversation, hoping for an inkling of enlightenment.

"We used to go out together after Nancy's divorce, but she became too possessive and I finally had to tell her to leave me alone. Unfortunately, she had decided she was my best friend and she stalked me for a while."

"Stalked you?"

"It's hard to explain, but yes."

"So, you believe she was one of the people who attacked us?"

"Yes, I think so."

"Mary, what would make you think that?"

Mary struggles with her answer, looking extremely distressed as tears dribble down her face. "I had an affair with her, but I'm not gay and I am not proud of what I did." As her shoulders cower down, she has a total breakdown. The waitress pretends not to notice as she drops off their tea. Beverly slows the conversation by pouring tea.

Gaining her composure, Mary continues: "Nancy and I were both brought up in the same church and divorce was something no one ever talked about. After her divorce, Nancy stopped going to church and claimed that she hated men. When I went through my divorce, she helped me through.

One day, she told me that if she were me, she would take my old wedding ring and have it made into an elegant piece of jewelry that was totally and exclusively mine. Because I was still hurting from my divorce and my X was asking for the ring, it sounded like great revenge, so I did it.

At work that week, everyone was asking me where I got my beautiful diamond necklace. It was so much fun that I went through all of the jewelry that past lovers had given me to express their 'true love' and picked out the best and most expensive ones to be made into new pieces that I could enjoy.

To make a long story short, in the past two years I have made myself quite a treasure of exciting jewelry with real stones from gifts I have received over the years from men who did not keep their promises."

Mary looks up long enough to see Beverly's face and throws out, "I know what you are thinking! I DID NOT steal Bob's X-wife's jewelry to make new jewelry!"

"Mary! I wasn't even thinking that! I was just baffled as to how this connects back to what happened that evening in the parking lot!"

Mary hides her eyes with her hands, but it cannot disguise the uncontrollable shaking of her shoulders. The restaurant is not busy, but several people are looking their way.

Beverly feels like she is on the edge of spilling the information she longs to know, "Mary, please! I need to understand what you think may have happened." Trying to avoid eavesdroppers, she adds in a low voice, "I'm really scared."

"Me, too." Mary responds, almost in a whisper. "But, I don't think we can talk here. Let's eat lunch and then go to your house, OK?"

Fear wells up in Beverly's gut, but she tries not to show it. Should she trust Mary? "Why don't we ask for our lunch to go? It's a nice day – we can eat at the park, OK?"

"Sure."

At the park, Mary seems much more relaxed and begins her story. "About a month after Ellen was killed, Nancy brought me a beautiful ring with many diamonds, including a large marquis. I did not even have an inkling of a thought that the stones could have come from Ellen and Anna's rings."

"Did you keep the ring Nancy gave you?"

"No. I had been trying to ditch Nancy, so I turned it down. I told Jennifer about the ring and she was the one who asked me if I thought the ring was made up of Ellen's wedding ring and Anna's eternity ring."

"Do you think it was?"

"I didn't at first. Cindy (the older cleaning lady) had started taking interest in my son and sometimes asked me to go shopping with her. What I did not know was that she was one of Nancy's lovers. One day she showed up angry on my doorstep, asking me if I was having an affair with Nancy. I told her that I had not seen Nancy in weeks. It was then that I noticed the ring on Cindy's finger. She noticed my stare and she scared me out of telling anyone by saying: 'Stay away or you know what can happen!'

Her threat really frightened me and it was then that I began to wonder if Jennifer was right about the ring. Cindy and Nancy both work in our building as janitors, they could have known both Ellen and Anna and about their rings."

"Do you think the rings could be motive for murder? That just seems so petty . . ."

"I'm not sure, but yes, I think the rings *and jealousy* have something to do with both murders. I believe that Nancy became jealous of my affair with Bob and either killed Ellen or had her killed to hurt Bob. Nancy took Ellen's ring as a souvenir. You have to understand that the rings represent a hatred for lost love."

Beverly is shocked to have confirmation that the affair between Mary and Bob was taking place before Ellen died. Mary seems oblivious and continues, "Nancy felt that all I wanted was bigger diamonds, but what I really wanted was to be loved! How could she even think that I would leave Bob for her?"

Beverly cannot believe that two people would be killed just so that a woman could vie for Mary's attention. "Why do you think Anna was killed?"

"My theory is that Anna saw Nancy and Cindy come out of the restroom. They had to kill her to keep her quiet and just took her ring as a bonus."

"So, you believe Cindy was also involved?" Beverly asks.

"Yes. I think they did it together."

In her mind, Beverly adds to the drama that she believes that Nancy and Cindy must have threatened Anna before she was murdered. Why else would she have a gun in the drawer? Guilt for not telling the authorities about the gun engulfs Beverly once more.

"You believe me, don't you?" asks Mary.

Beverly answers with a question, "If what you say is true, how would we prove it? We cannot tell the authorities until we have something concrete."

"I know . . . Beverly, I know that I have done a lot of things wrong in my life. I have done so many things that I don't even feel comfortable in church, which really confounds my mother.

The truth is that I really do believe and I want to be a better person for myself and my son. A n d I really do love Bob. I'm hoping that I can marry him, take care of our children and redeem myself somehow."

"Mary, I do understand, but you can't redeem yourself. Only Jesus can do that. Does Bob go to church?"

"Yes, but he is a different religion."

"I am not sure that matters. Become the best person you can be and I guaranty that God will hear you."

"He has not heard me so far."

"Do you mean he has not given you what you want? I used to see things that way, too, but you know what? Jesus died on a cross. Does that mean that the Father did not hear him? If every prayer was answered, it would be so easy to live a good life! After all, life is only difficult when things are hard. We need to take each day what we are dealt and do the very best we can to live good lives and share God's love." Beverly does not usually speak of God in public and she feels like the speech came out so effortlessly that it was almost as though it was not she who said it.

The two battered women's eyes meet and each reaches out for the other. In each other's arms, they both break down and cry.

Then Mary says, "Let's do the best we can to bring whoever is responsible for Ellen and Anna's death to justice. That would be good for us, their families and our families. What do you think?"

"I'm with you, Mary, but we need a plan."

Chapter 22: Communication Melt Down

Bill and Beverly linger in silence at the dinner table. The kids are hibernating in their rooms. For the past several weeks, the relationship has become strained with clouded feelings and buried secrets that have kept their souls hidden.

"Beverly, I need to talk to you about something," Bill starts. "I feel that we are good friends, but our relationship is not going anywhere. I know that you have been through a lot in the past year, but you have not really shared a lot of what you are thinking and feeling with me, especially since you left the hospital.

I thought that eventually things would get better, but they have not improved. For some reason, you will not or cannot share your life with me."

Beverly goes completely mute. She was not expecting this, especially not now! Tears do not hold back, even though she tries desperately to hide them. How can you ask someone to stay when your life is so filled with secrets and upheavals that you cannot share without appearing completely insane?

The uncomfortable silence causes Bill to lower his eyes. "We have never shared intimacy. At first, I thought it was because you needed time, but now I know that our relationship is definitely not progressing."

Beverly's silence becomes more deafening, but Bill continues, "I guess I'd better go. I won't be seeing you for a while, OK? I will call you sometime to see how you are doing, but right now I need some space." His voice now is showing outward stress, but Beverly's silence only assures him that he must go. He rises from the table, gets his coat and walks out the door.

Beverly starts to go after him, but when the door shuts, all she can do is run to her room and fall helplessly into a fetal position on the floor. She buries her head in her arms, trembling and crying hysterically. There is no one there to notice. The night wears on as she torments herself with inner conversations and prayers for strength that she has no faith will come.

At 2:00 a.m., her tears have completely burned out, so she quietly moves from room to room, checking on each of her children, who all sleep peacefully. She lays her hands on each in prayer, asking God to protect and watch over them.

Finally back in her own room, she bravely turns off the light, covering her head with the covers to keep out whatever evil lurks in the darkness. Sleep compassionately takes her away until she is rudely awakened by the alarm clock at 6:30 a.m. Because it is Saturday, she lays in bed awake for another half hour, but she cannot resume her sleep. She dresses quietly and heads out the front door for a walk.

The streets are silent, except for an occasional early riser driving by. Cool air softly blows her face as she breaks into a run. After just a short sprint, she feels her age and slows down.

The adrenalin gives her a backward glimpse of the happiness she knew early in her marriage when she was young and hopeful. Longingly she remembers her young children laughing hysterically as they rolled down hills of soft grass, dizzily rising and then falling down to laugh some more.

Was it all just a fantasy? The world seemed so good, all her prayers were prayers of thanks, and there were no haunting demons.

Her step quickens in an attempt to outrun her anxieties for herself, her kids, Bill, Mary, Bob – everyone she knows or cares about. What if God is just part of her utopian fantasy? *"Dearest Creator, are you there? If you are, would you please send a sign? I feel so alone!"*

The silence remains, her adrenalin soars, tears will not stop and there is no relief.

* * * * *

The night Bill gave his break-up speech and left Beverly's house, he went home and turned on the television, letting the distraction separate him from his feelings. The ploy worked minimally, and after a couple hours, he sighed loudly and turned it off. He could no longer filter out his thoughts.

It was hard to digest how the night had ended so abruptly. He had expected Beverly to stop him or at least to cry. But then, maybe he didn't give her a chance. He had been thinking about what he would say for weeks, but still it felt graceless when he said it out loud to her.

He rose from his chair and walked over to the window. The evening was quiet with a background of soft rain. The yard lights exposed muted outlines of his neatly manicured lawn. Streaks of light accentuated the cobblestone walks. Perhaps it was his mood, but all the trees and shrubs seemed to bend downward slightly, as if they were crying.

'I don't understand her, but I never really understood my X-wife, either. Maybe I just don't understand women in general.

Beverly seems to enjoy being with me, but she shows no capacity for romance. I don't know if she is becoming disinterested, was never interested, or is just so stressed out that she can't respond to me.

Why is her life so full of drama? Is it the way she lives her life or has she just had extremely bad luck?'

Moving to the bedroom, he opened a drawer full of miscellaneous photographs and took out a small handful from the top. Thoughtfully, he studied each one.

The first was a grand memory of his beautiful Melody's second birthday. She wore a sleeveless dress with yellow dots, her long blonde hair pulled back into a messy ponytail and perky front bangs. On her head was a pointed paper birthday hat and she was pushing her fingers into the cake with an impish smile on her face.

The next picture was a happy moment where he was with his son, Clifford, on a boat. Both were squinting at the sun as he held up a medium-sized red snapper dwarfed by the great big Cod fish that Clifford was holding. Clifford was smiling from ear-to-ear with his braces gleaming in the sun; his blonde hair in complete disarray; his pants with a large hole in the knee; and his flannel shirt open, displaying a green T-shirt with a superhero on it. Bill's white sailor's hat, unbuttoned white shirt and shorts portrayed relaxation that he has denied himself for years. Studying the picture more closely, he noticed that he sported a tight belly and handsome face that showed much less wear back then.

The third picture is the same day as the boat ride, because he is wearing the same outfit down to the hat. He is holding his smiling x-wife (Natalie) sporting short shorts and a mid-drift top, her light brown hair covered with a large woven hat and her eyes hidden with sunglasses. He held on to that picture for quite some time, feeling so close that for a moment in time he could smell the sea air and feel her soft hair blow into his face at a time when he was loved, comfortable with himself, and happy.

The last picture he held in his hand was of the entire family; him, Natalie, Melody and Clifford. This time they were all smiling, holding up pop cans like they were "toasting" each other and wearing matching plaid shirts and jeans. Both kids displayed braces and clear blue eyes.

He remembered the day as though it was yesterday. This was the day they celebrated his promotion to Director. Natalie had bought the shirts and made a special dinner of barbequed steaks, potato salad, and fresh vegetables with a chocolate layered cake for dessert. They ate outside in their stunning backyard with spring flowers in full bloom.

At the time, he had felt that the garden was much like his marriage, full of beauty today and promises for tomorrow. No longer able to hold back tears, he reached for a hidden treasure at the bottom of the drawer, a newspaper article with the headline, "8-Year-Old Boy Hit in Fatal Car Incident."

Slumped down to a clumsy sit-down position on the bed with head drawn forward in sorrow, he remembered that dreadful day when Natalie called him in hysterics to tell him that Clifford had been hit by a car while catching the baseball he got him for his birthday. He rushed to the hospital, but Clifford was already dead by the time he arrived.

Common sense told him that it was an accident and no one's fault, but he could not help but wonder how things would be had he not died. What if he had bought him a tackle box instead of a baseball?

Regardless, two parents numb with grief made preparations for a funeral for their beloved child. After the funeral, there was a deafening silence; silence that drifted two people apart. By the end of the following year, the barrier between them was so huge that he barely felt the pain when she told him she was in love with someone else.

It was not until they sat down and told their daughter that the numbness let loose and gave way to pain. By then it was too late. The worst part was that Natalie gave up custody of their daughter and only asked for visiting rights. It was as though she had completely forgotten how happy they once were. She then moved to Los Angeles and remarried, but has since moved back to Seattle to be closer to her daughter.

At that moment, a reality hit Bill in the head: Relationship is a conversation, so when the conversation stopped, Natalie and he were powerless to continue their marriage. Beverly's inability to communicate what is happening in her life has been destroying their relationship and sabotaged the conversation of love.

Now it all makes sense, but his worst fear in starting a new relationship was losing his heart and now he feels convinced the relationship is over and his heart is broken again. The comfort he sought trying to love again failed to materialize because the conversation stopped.

What is love, anyway? If it is a noun, then he has never seen it. If it is a verb, why do so many people choose to stop doing it? Perhaps for some it is just a metaphor for how you feel when you are infatuated and does not really exist at all. If it does exist, how do you stop loving someone you really care about?

With these thoughts and others haunting him through the night, Bill came to the realization that he does not stop loving. He still loves his ex-wife, his deceased son, his daughter, Beverly, and Beverly's children very much. Love does not turn off like a faucet for him.

In his middle age, Bill wondered if he no longer was attractive to women. Perhaps the belly and balding head are complete turn-offs. Perhaps Beverly only felt sorry for him and never saw him as more than a friend. With a sudden burst of anger, he threw the pictures back into the drawer and wiped away his tears with his shirt.

His life-story was now wide open and staring at him. He married a beautiful girl and loved her. They had two beautiful children. Clifford died. Natalie left him because he did not communicate well after Clifford died. Being Melody's dad became his focus. One day he met and eventually loved Beverly, but she does not seem to love him the way he loves her. *" Let the breakup be on her shoulders!"*

Still feeling an acutely sore lump in his throat, he quickly flicked off the bedroom light to retire to his bed to fight for sleep on a restless night. *'Who are you, God, that you torture me so? I thought Beverly was the one I would love forever, but you seem content to leave me empty-handed.'*

Chapter 23: Mysterious Calls That Frighten

Rain once again batters the roof at *Gerry's Socks & Shoes* as Beverly's heart stops for a moment to catch a glimpse of the woman she believes to be Nancy mopping at the top of the stairs. Looking a little more ragged than usual with her curly red hair in disarray, she looks up with an indignant look that freezes Beverly's heart. By the time Beverly gets to her cubicle, her heart is beating out of her chest.

Scanning email, she finds a message from Mary: "Beverly, please don't tell anyone what I told you. No one must know. Nancy will be caught in due time. This nightmare must go away! I love you! Mary."

Beverly cannot recall even a semblance of what she must do for the Company today and the eerie feeling in her gut makes work seem unimportant anyhow. A meeting notice flashes on her screen, so she dials into the meeting.

Tuning out, she clicks through email absent mindedly and is surprised to see Nancy looking straight at her when she glances up. Clumsily standing up and holding her headphones in place, Beverly catches Nancy looking back one more time as she walks by. The broken edge of fear scrapes on Beverly's heart.

She responds to Mary's email: "Don't worry. Your secrets are safe with me. Have you returned to work already or are you working from home?"

Almost immediately, Mary responds: "I am working from home, but don't worry, I am watching Nancy for you."

Like a reflex, Beverly snaps back, "Actually, she is watching me today and I am really scared."

"Don't worry. I have eyes everywhere."

Mary's answer spooks Beverly as she recalls the surveillance cameras. "Do you mean you actually can see her or that you have other people here watching her?"

"Of course I can't see her physically, Silly! Don't worry. Nothing bad will happen. I promise!"

Nancy walks by Beverly's cubicle again, but now heading in the opposite direction. This time she only stares at the floor.

The phone meeting ends and Beverly has no idea what was discussed. Nancy's face is engraved in her mind. Nature calls, but fear keeps her glued to her seat. She longs to call Bill and tears well up in her eyes as she realizes that she may have lost him.

She is deep in thought, when the phone rings. A low woman's voice says, "I know you don't know me, but I need to talk to you."

"Who is this?"

"You don't need to know that. There is someone that you believe is your friend who is not."

"How would you know this?" Beverly does not recognize the voice.

"She had you beat up."

"Who is this? Is this Nancy?" The caller hangs up.

A new email arrives from Mary: "Don't trust anyone."

Beverly surveys the ceiling and then begins searching her cube frantically. Finally, on the back of one of the pictures of her kids she sees what looks like it could be a tiny camera.

She looks away and pretends not to see it. Her heart complicates its beat as she slowly rises and heads out to the right from her cubicle, pretending to go to the break room. At the first hallway, she takes a left turn and sneaks off to an empty conference room.

Alone she contemplates the situation. Was it really a camera? What else would it be? It could have been a sound bug, but that would still mean that someone was spying on her. Fear pulls down on her. The physical shaking and red, hot face confirm her stress. She knows that sooner or later, someone will need the conference room where she is hiding, but her feet feel locked to the floor.

"One step at a time," she reminds herself as she formulates a plan. First she dials her manager's number from the conference room to tell her that she is suddenly feeling very ill and will need to go home for the day. Then she rouses up sufficient courage to make her getaway.

As she approaches her desk, she looks both ways to make sure no one sees her and drops down to her hands and knees to get her purse and keys from under her desk (to avoid being seen by the camera). She is not so graceful and her legs ache after crawling back to the hallway where she tries to stand up. Today was not the day to wear a dress. To her relief, the hallway remains clear and she does not believe anyone has seen her humiliating antics.

There are elevators in the back of the building that are rarely used (except when the two bodies were carried out of the building). She decides to go to the ground floor via the elevator, to avoid being seen on the stairs.

Beverly's eyes dart around wildly, looking for hidden cameras, wondering if she is making some fatal error in her escape plan. On the main floor, she chooses the front door exit where the security guards reside, rather than the unguarded side exit. She calculates the risk as she fumbles around for her keys before exiting the building into the pouring rain.

Halfway home, she decides to turn around and go to her mother's house and tell her the entire story. When she arrives, she sits in front of the house for some time, realizing her stupidity. Her mother is at work right now, like most women under 70 who are not wealthy.

After applying some hefty self-sympathy, Beverly heads for a fast food restaurant, bypassing the order desk to get to the restroom where she does her business and then breaks down in long, silent sobs, sitting in the stall.

Does God hear prayers sent while one is sitting on the toilet? Wiping her nose in a filthy public restroom with torn and ragged toilet paper that was touching the floor, she finds herself asking questions that she cannot answer. She wonders if this is insanity and if so, what will become of her?

In her unlikely place of refuge, she bargains with God vehemently until she is interrupted by the steps of an intruder entering the bathroom. She quickly pulls her clothes back on, flushes, and leaves in a hurry without even washing her hands. Heading off into the downtown Seattle streets, she wonders aimlessly, letting the rain drench her completely and refusing to protect herself from the cold.

'Perhaps I will never go home or to work again,' she muses to herself. Time stands still and the world seems to move in rhythm to her stride down the steep hill towards the seashore. Between the tall office buildings she sees battered fishing boats bobbing in the sea about two blocks away and smells the salty aroma of fish and seaweed in the air. Walking toward the drenched beach, she observes people going in and out of beachfront businesses, trying to keep dry with umbrellas blowing wildly and hats or newspapers on their heads to protect them from the storm. Beverly contemplates how worthless it is to cover oneself in such a storm, because regardless of the protection each person attempts to enact, they are all still hopelessly wet.

Compelled by her own thoughts to keep walking, Beverly's hands are now cold and numb. A tall man with a bald head runs to his car with two rag muffin boys that sport mops of longish, blonde wet hair. Seagulls walk along the sidewalk picking up garbage. Hours disappear and the sky darkens before Beverly realizes that she must go home to her kids, even though the sweet voice of death is calling her by name.

Chapter 24: Menacing Phone Calls & Fireworks

"Where have you been? Don't you think we worry about you?" Jason demands, standing at the door with his hands on his hips and looking very angry.

"IS MOM HOME, YET? The phone's for her!" Tania yells from her room.

Jason walks off, looking very disgusted. Although Beverly feels remorseful for worrying her kids, she dreads the phone call. It is either her boss who found out she was not ill or that dark voice she suspects was Nancy. "Hello?"

"Hello! Just wondering how you are."

It's Bill!

"I . . . I'm fine. How are you?" Beverly asks in a soft voice, on the verge of tears.

"I'm fine, but I'm worried about you. What I said the other night was not to end our friendship. I don't know . . . maybe you feel differently . . ."

"Bill, honestly it's not you. I think that I am falling apart at the seams. There seems to be no one I can trust . . ." Beverly's voice is faltering.

"You can trust me."

"I know." The silence hurts.

"Are you sure you are OK? The kids called me and said you were late home from work and wanted to know if you were here."

"I got a weird phone call today that scared me to death."

"Did you call the police?"

"No."

"Why not?" His voice has turned angry, a part of him that she has never experienced before. "If someone is harassing you, then you need to let someone know! Honestly, Beverly, I cannot understand why you have not been seeking help for all of the stress you are under. A person cannot function under so much pressure. You are pushing away the people who love you!"

"I don't need counseling. I just need for it to stop!" Beverly chokes.

Bill is silent for a moment and then asks, "Would you like for me to come over for a while?"

"Would you please?" Beverly asks and then realizes that she NEEDS for him to come over.

She hangs up the phone and surveys the messy living room. Her instincts start her on a cleaning frenzy to do a complete house makeover before Bill gets there, but the phone rings again.

"MOM, IT'S FOR YOU AGAIN!" Tania informs.

Beverly answers hesitantly, "Hello."

"Where have you been? I need to talk to you!" a familiar, raspy voice demands.

"Is this Nancy?"

"You don't need to know who this is. You don't know Mary like I do. She is very dangerous and you are in danger."

"She says you are dangerous." Beverly's heart is skipping beats and she feels as if a dark evil spirit is invading her body, suffocating her life away.

The voice retorts, "You trust the wrong person. If you don't believe me, watch what happens next." She hangs up.

Beverly immediately dials for the number of the last call received, but the automated voice line tells her that the number is blocked. Should she call the police? What would she tell them? Would they believe that the person she believes beat her called her today and told her to watch out for Mary? Even to Beverly that seems bizarre – and who is to say that the voice is Nancy's? She never identified herself and the voice sounded like it was disguised.

The phone in Beverly's hand rings and practically sends her through the ceiling. "Hello?" She hears Tania, who answered at the same time, and listens in for a moment to see who it is.

"Hi, Beverly. This is Mary," Mary sing-songs.

Tania hangs up loudly, causing Mary to ask, "Did you just hang up on me?"

"That was Tania; she thought it was for her. How are you, Mary?" Beverly does not want to talk to Mary right now.

"I'm fine, but you left work early – are you OK?"

"Yes, I had a dentist appointment." Beverly lies.

"Oh. I just wanted you to know that I went to the police today and told them what I suspected about Nancy. They are going to investigate. When they call you, please tell them everything you know."

"I don't really know anything."

"Sure you do! You know it was Nancy!"

"I don't know that."

"Beverly, you told me that you did know it was her."

"No, you said that you thought it was her. I don't know who it was."

"Who else would it be?"

"I don't know. Listen, Mary, I have a guest coming in a few minutes and need to straighten up the house, would you call me tomorrow sometime? We can talk then."

"Uh . . . I suppose so. I just wanted you to know that the detectives will probably be contacting you. Nancy will go to jail and we will both feel safer. Won't that be great? I'll call tomorrow, OK?" The sweetness in her voice makes Beverly's stomach turn. Could she really be that dumb?

"OK. Bye, Mary."

"Bye."

When Bill appears, Beverly tells him about the calls from "Nancy" and he tells her that she should tell the police in the morning. Then he makes a gesture that Beverly is relieved for, even though she feels totally undeserving. He offers to spend the night on the couch and go with her to the police in the morning. They put on a "chick flick" and Beverly falls asleep long before it is over in the warmth of Bill's arm.

Halfway through the night she awakes and starts to get up, but Bill, already awake, holds her tightly with his arm. "Shhhh." He says and she stops to listen.

In the silence of the night, she can hear footsteps to the porch and a car running in the background; the sound of something dropping; footsteps running away and the sound of a car taking off. Before Beverly and Bill have time to get up, there is a huge explosion on the porch.

They rise from their safety to see fireworks going off on the porch. One blast hits the door window and cracks it. The noise insults their ears and the kids come running from their rooms.

Once the noise stops, Bill goes out to survey the damage. There is not much, but the ground is littered with paper and debris. The neighbors across the street are standing in their pajamas looking out the door.

"It's ok! Just some kids playing pranks," Bill yells over to them. They wave and go back inside.

Bill calls 911.

Chapter 25: After the Fireworks

Detective Simmons demands, "Why didn't you call me when you got the first call?"

Beverly hadn't yet even told her about Mary's email or the camera that she believes is on her desk. What if the camera was her imagination? Paranoia is a disease, you know. "The person on the phone did not identify herself and I felt that there would be nothing really to report."

"So, you have no idea who it was."

"I thought it could be one of our cleaning ladies -- Nancy."

"What made you think that?"

Dare she tell? "Well, Mary told me that she thought that Nancy was the person who beat both her and me up last month."

"What makes you think that what happened to Mary and what happened to you were related events?"

"I guess I never thought that they were not related."

"Do you talk to Mary often?"

"Yes. She is a co-worker and . . . friend."

As the detective writes her notes, Beverly surveys the detective's office, which is cluttered with scattered files stacked up high in several places on her desk, as well as on the floor to her right. Her computer screen-saver is showing a rolling marquee in bright, blue letters that says, "REALITY IS HOME, COMFORT, and COFFEE." She is taking notes by hand.

Her voice softens a little as she says: "You will need to call your insurance agent and have him coordinate with us before trying to do a damage check. Officers are there now collecting evidence and we do not want anyone to disturb the integrity of the site until they finish. Do you have a place where you and your kids can stay for the day?"

"I have family in the area."

"OK. Can you think of anything else that might help us?" Simmons says.

"Well . . . There is one more thing that I feel funny bringing up, but I guess I should."

"What's that?"

"I think there was a camera – or bug -- on my desk yesterday, on a photograph that I have of my kids."

"What do you mean you think? Did you see it or not?"

"I think so, but I wasn't sure. That is why I left for the day. I thought I was being watched."

"We'll look for it. Let me get an officer over there." She immediately dials her phone. "Hey, Doug. Would you send an officer over to *Gerry's Socks & Shoes* and look for a camera or bug on Beverly Scott's desk? Thanks!"

She then turns to Beverly and says, "Please take care of your personal business today and do not go to work. You look very tired. Do you need me to call your employer?"

"No. I will call them . . . On second thought; maybe you should call them, too. I called out sick yesterday."

"I will. You call me if you think of anything else, OK?"

"OK." All Beverly can think of is that she has kids who are scared and Bill thinks her life is outrageous.

When she walks out of the detective's office, Bill, who was also questioned about the incident, rises from his chair and immediately puts his arm around her. They walk in total silence until Bill finally says: "Do you and the kids need a place to stay?"

"Just for tonight."

"Then you should stay at my house."

"All of us?"

"I'll take you to the house, go to work, and then get the kids from school. I should be able to take the rest of the day off."

"Why are you so good to me?"

"Because I love you."

"I love you, too," Beverly responds, feeling more intensity in her words than ever before. Tears now fall down her face uncontrollably, but Bill is stoic.

He helps her into his car and they head off to his house. On the way home, Bill decides that he will also take the day off, so they both call their bosses and then Beverly calls the insurance agent.

Bill and Beverly spend the rest of the day trying to understand what has happened and who is involved. Beverly attempts to tell the story from beginning to end, but as she tells it she realizes how much of the story includes speculations rather than facts.

They work together on theories of what could have happened, possible motives, and the people who might be involved. Some of what they come up with seems far-fetched, which makes them laugh, but they continue to think out loud and enjoy the conversation. Bill consoles her and she tells him she is sorry that she felt that she could not burden him with all she was going through. Secretly, she knows that if she told him EVERYTHING, he would believe she was insane.

A three o'clock, Bill leaves to go get Beverly's kids from school. While he is gone, she finds herself dozing off in a large, overstuffed chair.

That evening, Bill and Beverly make dinner together, a vegetable stir fry with cut-up pork and rice on the side. When it is time for bed, Beverly's kids all make up bed roles to sleep on the floor; Beverly takes the couch by choice; and Bill and Melody each sleep in their own rooms.

Bill and Beverly have the same prayer that night, thanking God for keeping them safe and letting them love each other for now as very best friends. Perhaps tomorrow will bring more, but for today, that is enough.

Chapter 26: Following Suspicion

"Are you OK?" It's Mary, finally back in the office after two weeks of recovery. It is still hard for Beverly to look at her face, but her wounds are healing and makeup hides the worst of it.

Beverly is browsing email as she answers, half-heartedly, "Yes."

"I heard what happened to your house."

"There was not much damage and the insurance will cover it."

Mary leans in close, "Do you think Nancy did it?"

"I have no idea," Beverly retorts, disgusted that Mary will not leave her alone.

"She'll be found out soon enough." Mary says as she watches Beverly work on her email. Finally taking the hint that Beverly does not want to talk, she ends by saying, "Don't worry. They'll catch her."

The phone rings. It's Detective Simmons. "I just wanted you to know that we did not find a camera or bug anywhere on your desk. How are you holding up?"

"We're fine. I could swear I saw it there – the camera, I mean."

"I suppose it could have been removed."

Now Beverly feels sure that she is losing her mind as she remembers crawling out of her cubicle trying to avoid being seen by a bug that may not have even been there. Looking at the picture, she really is not sure she ever saw it at all. For the rest of the day she concentrates on nothing but catching up on her work. At ten minutes to five o'clock, she packs up her things to leave. She looks up to see Mary waiting for her.

"Are you ready to go?" Mary asks.

"Just about."

They walk out together. Outside the skies are overcast, but there is no rain. Mary tries to chitchat. As they walk toward Beverly's car, Mary passes up her own car.

"Mary," Beverly says firmly, "you don't have to follow me to my car."

"I know. I just thought you might want company."

"Thanks, but I'm fine on my own, OK?"

"OK."

As Beverly unlocks her car, she sees Mary heading off towards her own car. Fear creeps up on Beverly as she contemplates that someone could have put a car bomb in her car.

Mary drives by and seeing Beverly is not yet in her car asks, "Did you forget your keys?"

"No, I'm fine. Bye!" Beverly says quickly, opening her car door and feeling relieved when nothing happens. She starts up the car and drives away.

To her surprise, somehow Mary is behind her. To lose her, Beverly turns towards the ocean, which is the opposite way that both Mary and she need to go to get home. Mary follows.

For miles Beverly drives the wrong way, but each time she looks back, Mary is there. Making a couple quick turns, Beverly finally feels she has lost Mary, so she parks in a shopping center parking lot. Before she can pull her thoughts together, Mary pulls into the same lot and parks beside her.

Mary gets out of the car and comes toward Beverly's car. Beverly rolls down the window.

"Are you shopping, too? What a coincidence!" Mary says.

Beverly is not amused. "Are you following me?"

Mary laughs, "No, of course not!"

"I took a wrong turn. See you tomorrow!" Beverly responds cleverly, backing out with Mary standing just a little too close to the car.

On the freeway Beverly feels triumphant and safe, but as she exits the freeway, she looks into her rearview mirror and is shocked to see Mary. She, obviously, was not shopping and now Beverly is sure she is following her. Beverly heads for Bill's house, but when she gets there, she can no longer see Mary.

In the house, Bill, his daughter and her kids are making dinner, as they had planned the night before. "Hi. Hope you like spaghetti!" Bill greets her.

Beverly barely acknowledges them as she surveys the street from the front window. "What are you looking for?" Bill asks.

"This is going to seem silly, but I think Mary was following me today."

"Why would she follow you here?"

"I don't know."

Bill looks at her in silence for a moment, then sighs and returns to the kitchen to help the kids. Beverly continues to watch out the window. When she finally comes in the kitchen, Bill and she avoid the subject of Mary following her. Later that night, as the local news raps up on the TV, Bill suggests that because it is Friday, they should have a movie night.

One by one, the kids doze off on the floor and Melody goes to her room. Bill covers each of Beverly's kids with a blanket and takes Beverly's hand to lead her to the bedroom. "I'm sorry, Bill, I have kids in the house," Beverly says softly.

"I know," he replies, "but, I don't believe it would be any different if they were not here." His face reflects a deep sadness, but she doesn't know what to say. She feels total remorse for her goody-two shoes right now, even though she knows that this is definitely not the time to sanctify a serious relationship in her life.

Letting go of Beverly's hand, Bill heads off to take his place on the couch. "You can have the bed," he says. Not wanting to argue or wake up the kids, Beverly complies quietly without explanation.

Chapter 27: Contradicting Testimony

Anger encourages Beverly as she heads for Mary's desk on Monday. "Why were you following me on Friday?"

"I wasn't following you."

"Yes, you were."

"OK. I just wanted to make sure you made it home OK, but you went to someone else's house."

"Don't EVER do that again!"

"Whatever."

Back at her own desk, anger still prevails over Beverly's spirit. The phone rings.

"I really need to talk to you." It is *that* voice again.

"Why do you need to talk to me?"

"Because Mary is trying to pin a murder on me and I did not do it."

"Who is this?"

"My name is Cindy. I work as a janitor here. Please hear me out. Would you meet me somewhere?"

Remembering what Mary told her about Cindy and despite her gut singing 'BEWARE!' Beverly answers, "Where can we meet?"

"I'll get my lunch at McDonalds and then we can meet at the park. It's so chilly today that I don't believe many people should be there. Would you meet me there at 11:30?"

"Sure. Is there a specific place you want to meet at the park?"

"Meet me near the woman's bathroom."

Bathrooms are not Beverly's favorite place, but there are not many landmarks in the park and all she wants is to understand what is going on. She is aware this could be a trap and worries about it all morning.

At 11:40, Beverly is sitting on a bench, damp from the slow drizzle of rain. In the distance she sees the older woman with grey-brown hair coming towards her with the hood of her dowdy black jacket held tightly around her neck by a clenched hand, apparently trying to keep dry.

She acknowledges Beverly with large brown eyes and sits down beside her. "I was really scared you would not be here," Cindy begins, her dark eyes meeting Beverly's.

"What is going on?" Beverly asks, fear gripping her heart as she realizes her solitude with this woman whom she knows nothing about.

"It's a very long story," Cindy begins with a sigh, her dark eyes staring down. "First of all, I want you to know that I am sorry for what happened to you. The attack, I mean."

Beverly's fear intensifies, but she bravely pushes for the truth, "Why did you attack me?"

"I'm telling you, it was Mary and a thug."

"If Mary had a thug beat me, why was she beaten?"

"I have no idea. Maybe she and the thug got into a fight or something."

"What? I'm sorry, I don't have time for this," Beverly says, gathering her purse to leave.

"Please stay!" Cindy looks sincere. "I don't know who did it, but let me tell you what I do know."

"I met Mary at a club and you will probably be shocked to know that I felt that she was the epitome of everything I ever wanted in a lover. She seemed so beautiful and sensitive. She and her son spent a lot of time with me and I was convinced we would be together forever. (Her little boy, Ivan, is a living doll!) Then one day I found out she was seeing someone else – that big, 'going somewhere' director guy that she is engaged to now. It's just like her to go for the money!"

The pause is too long and Beverly's curiosity is now active, but Cindy obviously dances to her own drummer. Her eyes rarely make contact, her large hands have no animation, and her speech is slow and gruff. After another large sigh, she grumbles, "When I confronted Mary about her relationship with Bob, she said that he was rich and could care for her and her son! She always goes for rich men who give her big rings and then she just takes the booty and leaves!"

Beverly is pretty sure that Mary's relationship issues are more that she chooses the wrong men, but she chooses not to share that with Cindy. The silence again ensues and Beverly's patience runs low, "Why would Mary go through the pain of a relationship just to take a ring?"

"Oh, it's silly really. A lot of us who hang together have had really bad experiences with men, so we kind of pride ourselves with taking expensive stones out of jewelry given to us by unsavory men and having them mounted into 'special' jewelry pieces for ourselves. Mary became the jewelry queen, because she has had so many past lovers with loads of money."

Beverly's heart is thumping much too hard as she remembers Mary's jewelry. "So, who took Ellen's ring?"

"I am not sure, but I think Mary hired someone else to kill Ellen and get her ring. At first, I thought she did it just for the ring, but now I believe it was so she could marry Bob."

"Why do you think that?" Beverly asks, feeling sick as this theory coincides with her worst fears.

"Well, after the murder, Mary started acting strange. We still had a couple dates, but then she stopped seeing me altogether. I felt so sad about it that I kept calling her. Finally, she asked me stop calling. I was so hurt, but not shocked, because we had never slept together." Cindy is now dripping tears and Beverly cannot help but have sympathy for this older, oversized, burly woman who seems to be telling the truth as she sees it.

Cindy continues, "Mary said that you told Anna that she was going to kill her and that scared Anna so bad that Anna killed herself. She said that you did it in revenge because you wanted Bob. She said she was planning to get a confession from you, but didn't tell me how. Right after that, you were attacked."

Now Beverly believes Cindy is fibbing, "You knew Anna?"

"Yes. It's complicated. Anna came to the Club once when Mary was with Nancy. I really liked her and tried to get her to like me, but she made it clear that she felt uncomfortable with us and left. We are not a crowd that everyone appreciates.

Mary then told us all that Anna was married, which makes me believe we probably scared her to death, because we are a tough crowd! That night, Nancy and Mary got into a fight and I took Mary home. That is when Mary and I started being friends."

"Was Nancy OK with that?" This is a world Beverly does not know or understand and she cannot quite get her arms around what is fact and what is fabrication.

"You're psyched out, right? I know it is not the way most people live, but most of the time it makes me happy," Cindy responds, feeling a bit more comfortable, which is witnessed by a little smile.

"Nancy was not ok that I took up with Mary, but as I told you, it only lasted a couple weeks."

"All this does not make much sense. Why are you telling me this anyway?"

"Because I believe that Mary went to the cops and told them that Nancy and I are Ellen's murderers. We have been called in several times for questioning and sometimes we feel we are being followed. I'm really getting scared!"

"Have you told the police what you told me?"

"I have tried, but I don't have any evidence that would be of any use to them. But, there is something else . . ."

"What's that?"

"After you were beat up, Mary told us she knew it was us and that she was going to find out if you knew, too. Later, she told us you were accusing us, too. That night, your house was bombed. Nancy and I were called in for interrogation for the bombing! We believe Mary told them that we did it!"

"Um . . . my house was not bombed. Someone set off fireworks on the porch. There was not much damage. It could have been teenagers."

"Yes, we just say bombed." Cindy falls to silence again.

Beverly ponders this conversation. With her head hanging low and tears in her eyes, Cindy seems more like a kitten than a tiger, but didn't Mary cry, too? How do you evaluate sincerity? Whom do you trust?

The rain-drizzle has thinned down to a fine mist touching the women's faces as they contemplate their encounter. Finally, Beverly asks, "If everything you have told me is true, what do you want for me to do?"

"I think we can trap Mary with her own game."

"How?"

"We will have to play the game with her. I will tell her that you are telling the police that she is the murderer and I believe she will send her henchman after you."

"That's nuts. I have three children at home. Why can't we just go to the police?" Beverly plays along.

"It would be our word against hers and they would not move unless there was another crime."

Beverly sees humor in this, "So, if I risk my life, all of this will be cleared up?"

"No! We would protect you and your children!"

"We who and how?"

"Haven't you figured it out? Mary has been spying on all of us with video cameras. We would do the same to protect you!"

"Like the ones that breached company security a few months ago?"

"That may have been her, too. I don't know. All I know is that she learned how to use them a while back to spy on Bob."

"Did she tell you that?"

"Yup. She used to share a lot with me," Cindy replies, thoughtfully. "I know what we'll do! I'll get a camera to spy on you; you tell Mary that I have told the police that she is the murderer; and when she tries to murder you, I will catch her on camera and call the police."

"That seems very risky to me."

"Do you have a better idea?"

"Yes, go to the police and tell them what you know."

"I thought you would say that, because it would be no skin off your nose if Nancy and I got blamed for it all."

Sitting in awkward silence, they both know that lunch hour is over and neither has a clue what action to take from here. "I've got to go," Beverly ends the conversation as she leaves Cindy on the bench alone.

"Mary will murder us both and no one will ever know the truth!"

The words from Cindy worry Beverly. As she heads towards the parking lot, she is more troubled to see a car that resembles Mary's. Stopping in her tracks, she searches for a place to hide and chooses a large bush to hide behind.

From what she can tell from a distance, the car is empty. Suddenly she feels ridiculous; because she is not really sure it is Mary's car. After much consideration, she decides to return to the bench to ask Cindy if she saw Mary's car.

As she nears the bench, she hears two women fighting in whispers. Taking a new hiding place among the trees, Beverly tries to hear what is being said, but finds that she is not close enough. Abruptly, a gun-shot-like blast assaults her ears and Mary suddenly dashes by, oblivious to Beverly in her hiding place.

Shocked, Beverly contemplates what to do next. She does not have the strength or courage to go see if Cindy is dead. After several

143

minutes, she is relieved to hear footsteps and finally see Cindy walking briskly after Mary. Beverly hardly breathes. She stays in her hiding place for a very long while. When she finally gathers the courage to edge towards the parking lot, only her car is left in the parking lot. She runs to it like a mad woman, fumbling with her keys to get it unlocked on the driver's side before she locks the door and tears out of the driveway.

What just happened? Beverly is not sure, but she heads back to work, terrified of what lies ahead and knowing full well that she is heading right back to the source of her fears, *Gerry's Socks & Shoes*. Every step she takes brings more panic as she heads back up the stairs and down the hall to her cubicle.

At her desk, she immediately notices a hand-written note in an unfamiliar hand that reads, "Beware of friends who would kill you."

Finally! Here in her hands was a shred of evidence that she could take to the police! She quickly writes an email to her boss that she must leave for the day for "personal reasons," picks up the note and heads out the door feeling like she has won the lottery.

* * * * *

Unfortunately, Detective Simmons is not as impressed with Beverly's evidence as she suspected she would be. "So, do you believe that the murderer put the note on your desk or one of the women you saw in the park?" she mocks.

"I honestly don't know." Beverly responds shamefully.

"Let's just suppose the women in the park had something to do with either one of the murders, how would this note help us to clarify that?"

"I don't know."

The detective shows a little pity when she says, "We could look for signs of a gunshot in the park, I suppose, but even that is unlikely, because it appears that no one was shot and nothing was reported."

"This note is threatening to me and I am afraid for my life." Beverly responds desperately. "Can't you, at least, find out who wrote it from the handwriting?"

"We may have examples of Mary and Cindy's handwriting in our records. I will have our staff look at it, OK? However, I cannot let you know who wrote it or make any judgment upon the person who wrote it. Writing a note that does not make specific threats is not a crime."

"I understand."

* * * * *

The house is as empty as Beverly's spirit when she finally arrives home. There is a note on the coffee table from Mark that he is at a friend's house and has been invited to dinner. He neglected to include a phone number, but at least he left a note.

Beverly looks around, but Tania and Jason are not home either and she has no idea where they have gone. She reminds them over and over again that she needs for them to keep her informed when they go places, but it is not unusual for either of them to forget. She feels anxious that she does not know where they are, but there is a lot more weighing on her right now.

The dark skies cast a grey tone on the front room, mimicking Beverly's feelings. She now believes that no one will ever know who killed Ellen, why Anna died, or who tried to kidnap or kill her – or whatever they were trying to do!

Her eyes no longer cry, but the darkness she feels under them exhausts her. Curling up in her favorite chair, she drifts off to a restless sleep where dreams play out her fears.

Too soon she awakes to hear the Jason and Tania coming in the front door. "Where have you been?" she greets them.

"I told you I was going the basketball game!" Jason blurts out in an exaggerated manly voice.

"I'm sorry, I forgot. Where have you been, Tania?"

"I went to study at Anne's house and I did call your work phone, but you were not there. I guess I should have called your cell phone. Sorry."

"What are you doing?" Jason asks Beverly as she dizzily stands up from the chair.

"I just wasn't feeling well." Beverly responds.

"So where's dinner?"

"You will have to eat the leftovers in the fridge. I had no idea where you were and Mark is eating at a friend's house. How was the game?"

"We lost."

While Jason is digging around in the refrigerator, Beverly turns on the TV just as her cell phone rings. It's Bill. "Do you need company?"

"I would like some."

Mark arrives home just a little before Bill arrives. Jason comes out of his room and asks, "I am so hungry. Don't we have anything else to eat?"

"I thought I just heard you heating something up!" Beverly responds, feeling a little guilty.

"Boys are always hungry," Bill laughs. "How about I order pizza?"

"I already ate." Mark says.

"Pizza would be good," Jason says hoping Bill won't change his mind.

Bill quick dials his cell phone and orders pizza. Comfort envelops Beverly. She cuddles up with him on the couch and watches the news on TV. When the pizza arrives, she finds solace listening to her kids happily banter with Bill while they all pig out – even Mark.

The night ends with a kiss and a huge hug. "I do love you, Bill. Please give me time to get through this."

"I love you, too, so I don't believe that I have a choice."

It is only 9:30 p.m. Beverly goes to her bedroom and stares at her cell phone. Finally, she decides to make the call.

"Hello?"

"Hi Mary."

"Hi . . ." Mary stutters, obviously disconcerted. "I . . . uh . . . didn't see you all day today."

"Really? Seems you and I both met the same person for lunch!"

"I don't know what you are talking about."

"You met Cindy at the park, didn't you?"

"Why would YOU meet Cindy at the park?"

"I could ask you the same question."

"If you are mad at me for something, why not just say so?"

"Who shot the gun?"

"What gun? Are you CRAZY? Honestly, Beverly, you need psychological help!"

"I heard a gun and you came running away from Cindy."

"Well, I was angry at Cindy and did hurry back to my car – mostly because I was already late back to work. But no one had a gun. Wait a minute – I think I did hear a car backfire!"

Did she say she heard a car backfire? Beverly scrambles for something to say. "It was not a very good day to go to the park, was it?"

"I thought I saw your car." Mary returns, matter-of-factly. "Are you friends with Cindy? I really did not know that. For Pete's sake –

why would you think one of us would have a gun? I was eating at a table on the other side of the park and just found Cindy sitting there. She was in a bad mood, so I just left."

"Did you leave a note on my desk today?"

"A note? About what?"

"Never mind."

"Beverly, why did you call me? Are you and Cindy seeing each other or something? You know what? I don't really want to know."

Beverly looks up to see Mark looking at her curiously. "No. Listen, Mary, I'll talk to you tomorrow, OK? I'm just tired."

"Whatever. I think you are really losing it, Beverly. See you tomorrow!"

"Bye."

Mary just hangs up.

"Are you OK, Mom?" Mark asks at the door.

"Oh! I was just talking to a friend."

"Your face is REALLY red. Are you sure you are ok?"

"I'm just not feeling well, but I will be ok. It's time for you to go to bed!" She gives him a hug and he heads off to bed. Beverly dials Bill's number.

"I was already missing you."

"Really? Did not expect that," Bill responds.

"Just wanted to say goodnight."

"Goodnight. Sweet dreams – and don't let the bed bugs bite!"

It is more than bed bugs bothering Beverly right now, but she keeps it to herself. How in the world did she get into this story? It was certainly not out of choice.

Chapter 28: Mary's Theory

In the drab cubical farm at *Gerry's Socks & Shoes*, there are speckled, yellowed acoustic ceilings that meet dingy white walls decorated with colorful framed prints of modern art. The partitions are a dated gray fabric with black and pink swirls that must have been someone's great idea for a 1950's "retro" pattern. The durable fabric shows little wear, so the cubical walls could last for posterity.

The scuttlebutt is that the Executives are considering a new office design with smaller cubicles that hold four workers in social "pods" with the promise of increased collaboration. Enticed by pretty pictures on embellished presentations, they fail to consider the loss of privacy, making simple things (like burps!) distractions and farts major catastrophes. Already some employees use the bathrooms to talk to their doctors. Who wants the world to know you need an appointment for female issues or a colonoscopy?

The stale smell of dusty carpet welcomes Beverly to work in the early morning. She admires the light from the window where liberated dust flutters on beams of sunlight. Other than the security guards at the front door, Beverly is fairly sure she is the only person working this early at Gerry's Socks & Shoes. Her cubicle is far from the windows and as she heads toward it, she notices the hallway has a light out and another is blinking obnoxiously.

Consciously keeping memories of murder and other atrocities out of her head, she sets to work immediately. She has been feeling very insecure about her job because she is behind and she knows she cannot afford to lose it.

The only sounds are the noisy air-conditioner and abrupt silence each time it clicks off, as well as the low buzz of the lights and the rapid melodic clicks of Beverly's keystrokes. By 7:45 a.m., co-workers begin filtering in and by 8:10 the normal sounds of the busy office are in full swing, but Beverly does not notice as she methodically works through her "to do" list.

Mary's voice down the hall interrupts Beverly's rhythm, but she ignores it and continues on with her work. When she continues to the hear the exaggerated baby talk, she peers over the cubicle wall to see the lovely Mary dressed in a deep red dress with red lipstick (much too dark for her coloring), looking more like she is going to a high school dance than working. She is noisily introducing a well-dressed, elderly woman to each person in the office. Beverly recoils back in her chair, recalling her humiliating call to Mary last night.

The sounds of Mary's giggle and introductions continue down the hall until Beverly realizes with irritation that she will soon need to be a team player and welcome this newcomer, who has now been identified to every person within hearing distance as Marilyn, Bob's new secretary. It is almost comical to hear each person act surprised and try to make small talk. As Beverly hears the introduction at Janine's desk next to hers, she decides to stand up and greet the inevitable with a hearty, "Hello, Marilyn! I'm Beverly."

"Hello. Nice to meet you," Marilyn responds in a low, almost manly voice.

"Marilyn will be Bob's new secretary," Mary explains cheerfully.

"Well, it's nice to meet you. . ." Beverly reaches out to shake hands, but as she meets Marilyn's eyes, her heart stands still. The eyes seem to see right through her and she feels a chill run down her spine. She gives a weak smile and is relieved when Mary moves on for the next introduction.

Beverly watches them walk on and wonders if what she feels is triggered by paranoia, intuition or a true memory. As usual, Mary seems totally oblivious to any change in the social climate, but Beverly does not miss that Marilyn's eyes stay focused on her until she sits back down in her cubicle. Staring down at her keyboard, Beverly again feels fear run up her back and grip at her heart.

What should she do? Detective Simmons would only roll her eyes if she went back after the "note" incident. Besides, Beverly cannot separate her true recollections from her daily haunting, which makes it difficult to recall a well-jelled picture of what really happened. With nothing concrete to take to the police, like a mouse in a maze, she feels danger that will not dissolve until she is liberated by the solution. She contemplates whether this well-dressed woman could have been one of the thugs who tried to kidnap her. The whole concept seems bazaar.

After all, Bob just hired her and this is her first day at *Gerry's Socks & Shoes*.

Beverly stands up slowly to get another look at Marilyn, who is now giggling with Mary at Toni's desk, the woman who took over Jennifer's position in the Company. If Marilyn did feel anything unusual when she met Beverly, she does not seem to have skipped a beat. Beverly feels that from a distance, she looks like a kindly, older woman, maybe in her late fifties or early sixties. She has full-grey hair that is a little long, but looks well kept.

At the *Gerry's Socks and Shoes* quarterly budget meeting, Bob proudly introduces his new sidekick (Marilyn) to the group. After the meeting, everyone gathers around Marilyn and Bob to welcome her and brown nose. Beverly exits the room quietly and returns to her desk.

She opens her email to find a message from Mary: "Would you have lunch with me today?"

Doesn't Mary get it? Beverly does not consider her a friend anymore! Just as Beverly is preparing to write back an excuse, she looks up to find Mary standing at her desk. "Hi," she manages to say, disquieted.

"Hi. I really need to talk to you. Can we have lunch?"

"Sure." Beverly responds without a smile, feeling angry.

"Cool. Is 11:30 too early? I know it is already past eleven."

"No. We can go now if you want. I'd like to have a longer afternoon to get things done."

"Thank you! Let me get my sweater!" Mary sounds relieved and somewhat excited.

In Beverly's car, Mary is a quiet passenger. It is obvious she knows that Beverly is angry. They go to what used to be their favorite spot, a small deli where they serve soup and sandwiches. After standing in line to order, they take their number to a table and sit down to wait for their food.

Mary starts the conversation with, "What did you think of Marilyn?"

"She seems OK. Why?"

"You are not going to believe this, but I know Marilyn from a club that I used to go to. But, the Marilyn I met today does not even seem like the same person. When I met her, she belonged to a motorcycle gang and was very tough and crude."

"Are you pulling my leg, Mary? That does not even seem possible," Beverly responds, wondering if Mary's lying is getting out of hand and where the heck THIS conversation is going.

"I know. I was in total shock when I saw her, but I understand that she has very good secretarial skills. Bob would not hire someone who was not of a high caliber." Mary is avoiding eye contact.

"Is this what you wanted to talk about?"

"Kind of . . . Listen, I know you are mad at me, but I really do still care about you." Her eyes meet Beverly's and she cannot help but believe her. "Maybe I am crazy, but I think Marilyn was Nancy's accomplice in the beatings."

"You know, Detective Simmons said she was not even sure if the two crimes were related – and I thought you thought it was Nancy and Cindy!" Beverly sternly reminds Mary.

"I just thought you may have recognized her," Mary says as her face drops down to hide the tears in her eyes. With desperation in her voice, she pleads, "Don't you understand? I need to figure out what happened and why or I will never feel safe again!"

Beverly collects her thoughts. "I understand, Mary. My life is in complete disarray because of all this crap going on. Marilyn did look familiar to me, but I don't know if I really remember her or if I have just become so paranoid that I have anxiety attacks over nothing. The more time that goes by, the less I seem to recall and the more I feel that I am fabricating half of what I believe I remember. It is almost as if it were all a dream!"

Mary is now very sober. "You seemed weird on the phone last night day. You don't think I murdered Ellen do you?"

"I don't have a clue who murdered Ellen."

Mary sighs. "You are going to think that I am nuts, but I have a theory."

"You are nuts," Beverly responds with a weak attempt at humor, "but no more than I am. What is your theory this time?"

"Actually, I did talk to Cindy the other day and what she said made me change my mind about what I believe happened. Do you remember when I told you about the affair I had with Nancy?"

Beverly nods, looking down to avoid her feelings about Mary's bi- sexuality.

"Well, I didn't tell you that I really kind of belonged to a whole group of girlfriends – and Marylyn was the leader of the group. We would meet up several times a week to man-bash and drink too much.

Sometimes I would come into work with a hangover or not come in at all, so I am really lucky that Bob did not fire me! When Nancy made her first pass at me, I was quite outraged at men in general and very vulnerable."

After a short pause with no response from Beverly, Mary continues, "Nancy proved to be more domineering and possessive than any man I have ever been with, though. When I began to realize that I really DID like men and that being with Nancy was not my dream, we had a very violent fight and broke up. She actually gave me a black eye! Remember? I told everyone in the office that Ivan accidentally hit me with his baseball bat."

Looking at Beverly for some kind of reaction or reassurance, Mary adds, "It was just a tough time in my life when I needed to find out who I am. Maybe you will never understand . . . "

Beverly does not understand, but all she wants is the rest of the story. "I want to believe you, Mary, and I do remember that black eye. What happened next?"

"Well, the women's group had this weird thing we were doing with all the precious jewelry that past lovers had given us. It was supposed to be our revenge. We would take the jewelry to a jeweler and have it made into new pieces and then we would go to the bar and wear it proudly.

It really was fun to drink and poke fun at our X's and because I have really bad luck with men, I had the most valuable jewelry of all! It was like I was a Rock Star and everyone would make a big deal about how beautiful and valuable my pieces were. What can I say? I liked the attention. It was a competition that I could win!"

Beverly studies her plate, obviously not amused. "So, where does Cindy come into the picture?"

"After I broke up with Nancy, Cindy tried to keep me in the group. She liked me and let me know that I was still welcome and she would protect me from Nancy. But, I would not feel comfortable with Nancy there, so I stopped going. Cindy was really nice and I regretted that I had to stop seeing her eventually, but she wanted a relationship that I was not interested in and I already had another relationship.

Marylyn was really upset that I stopped coming to carouse with the girls, but even more upset when she heard that Bob and I were having an affair. She and her gang of motorcyclists came by my apartment one night and told me that I was a traitor and only dating Bob for his money."

"So you were having an affair with Bob BEFORE Ellen died?" Beverly asks point blank.

Mary looks ashamed, "Yes. At first I thought that Nancy and Cindy killed Ellen to get back at Bob for taking me out of their group, because they both work at *Gerry's Socks & Shoes.* But when I talked to Cindy the other day, I began to realize that Cindy does not have the demeanor or the smarts to plan a murder, but she would do anything to protect Marilyn.

I think she might know that Marilyn was the brains of the operation and Nancy participated. She can't tell anyone, because she both loves and fears them. It's all very complicated.

In revenge, Marilyn and Nancy took Ellen's expensive ring so that I would not inherit it. Marilyn told Cindy to tell me that you did it to see my reaction -- maybe to find out if I knew anything. I have seen both Marilyn and Nancy violent with other women in the group. I am not the only person in the group who got a black eye."

Beverly cannot help but give an opinion, "Bob told me he really loved Ellen, so I don't understand why he was having an affair."

"Yes. I know it was not right, but not much has been right in my life the past two years! My mother says I am going to Hell."

"Why do you think Marilyn applied for a job as Bob's secretary?" Beverly plays along.

"I don't know, but I know she is probably up to something. I fear for myself, you, and Bob, but I don't know what to do!"

"You are not going to Hell."

A waitress comes to drop off their food, but neither Mary nor Beverly is hungry. Finally, Beverly pronounces, "Mary, I need for this whole thing to be resolved and the people involved put in jail. I need to trust you. Do you swear that you have told me everything that you know?"

"Well . . . there is a little more that I have remembered about the day I was beaten up. I had forgotten my laptop at my desk and drove back to get it. When I pulled my car into the parking lot, I saw some commotion in the darkness. For some reason, I felt no danger, so I walked toward the people instead of away. When they saw me, they began to run towards me and then when I saw the ski masks I realized that I could be in grave danger. As I was running away, I heard Nancy tell someone to 'get' me. At least, it sounded exactly like Nancy. My assumption has always been that because Cindy and Nancy work together, they must have been together that night. I went back to

Detective Simmons and told her what I remembered and that I thought it was Nancy and Cindy."

"But, now you think it was Nancy and Marilyn?"

"Yes."

"I thought that I recognized Marilyn's eyes as the same eyes that haunt me sometimes when I think of that night, but I really don't remember much."

"Really?!! Oh, Beverly, that would be the missing link if you could swear by it!"

"But, I can't. If it was Nancy and Marilyn, maybe they suspected I knew and set off fireworks on my front porch to scare me." Beverly pauses to formulate her thoughts as she begins to recognize the fear in Mary's eyes as the same fear she harbors.

Carefully, she puts together the question that will make or break her belief in Mary's story, "So, why were you following me that one day and how did you manage to meet Cindy in the park yesterday?"

Mary looks down and fidgets. "I go to the park often to walk. When I recognized both your car and Cindy's in the same parking lot, I was suspicious that you two had conspired together."

"You are kidding, right?"

"No."

"Would it surprise you if I told you that Cindy told me that you and a thug killed Ellen?" Beverly asks.

"Why would she say that?"

"To protect Marilyn?"

"Well, she lied to me, too, Beverly. She said you did it."

"So, why were you following me?"

"I wanted to know if you were meeting with Nancy."

"Why in the world would I do that?" Beverly asks in misbelief.

"Like you, I have been searching for the truth and not finding it."

Beverly now realizes that if Mary is telling the truth they are both sitting in the same boat rowing in opposite directions. Do they know enough collectively to solve the mystery of the two deaths? But who would ever believe either one of them?

Real life was beginning to feel as risky as it was for her imagined heroin in a book that she may never finish. As her heroin learned, reality does not end the way you wish it would, even if it results in heroic deeds and good for the masses. Nothing in life is as perfect as the child within you expected.

Mary then asks a question that Beverly is truly not expecting at all, "Beverly, do you pray?"

"Yes, I do."

"Tonight we should both pray for an idea of what we should do. I have just started going back to church with my mom, but it might take Him a while to forgive me. He might listen if we both pray. I always admire how good you are."

"I pray every day, Mary, but I know that if you have turned your heart to God, he does hear you, too. I am far from perfect and maybe not as good as you think. Remember that everyone has free will, so even God does not always interfere with those who want to do others harm.

We can only ask and hope that God sends us what we need when we need it, but it may not save us from what is to come. When things do not go right for me, I always remember that Jesus died on a cross." It seems very odd to be talking to Mary about prayer and even odder that the words come out so smoothly.

"I'll pray for our safety and peace of mind, Beverly. Thank you for taking me to lunch and we will figure this out."

Chapter 29: The Great Plan

Beverly's co-workers would be aghast to see her goody-two-shoes sporting ridiculously overt cleavage in a darkened bar featuring décor enhanced by sordid gang graffiti. There is a huge blackened skull on the ceiling with glow-in-the-dark green enhancements. Mice are depicted crawling out of the eye sockets and the teeth appear to be drawn up into a smile.

The silky red dress she is wearing is a little short, revealing too much leg, and a bit tight around her waist. Because she rarely even wears a dress (or even shorts) anymore, the bare-leg look only seems to over-emphasize that her thighs are thicker than they used to be. The extreme discomfort, however, does not outweigh her commitment to a greater purpose, something that she will do to make the world a better place live.

The smell of the sweet red wine in front of her calms her nerves, but she dares not drink too much. Stealing a sip of wine, she keeps her elbows plastered on the table, holding her cup in front of her and keeping her legs under the table to cover her nakedness as she eavesdrops on the many frivolous conversations around her.

Beverly has only sat in a bar a handful of times in her forty-plus years. But Mary, seated on her left, seems totally at home as she gaggles and giggles with her friends; three sharing the booth and two standing around her like flies to a picnic. She seems oblivious to any impending danger and Beverly wonders if she was the right partner to connive with for this highly important covert mission.

Marilyn barges through the front door with two other women, a bandana tied around her grey hair, her hefty breasts pushed high into a black, silver-studded leather vest. Beverly cannot help but be appalled at her hideous demonic tattoos, flabby arms, and bulging belly. She feels a fear far beyond what she has ever felt before. Seeing the transformation from stately executive secretary to this sordid identity is absolutely flummoxing, but amazing just the same. Not even the best Halloween costume Beverly has ever seen could transform a person so thoroughly.

Mary quietly acknowledges to Beverly that she has already seen Marilyn with her eyes and a nod, but her next bold move shocks Beverly, leaving her wondering if she should run for her life! Mary points in Marilyn's direction and says to everyone around the table, "Look, there's Marilyn!" She hops out of her chair like a school girl and heads directly towards Marilyn with her friends in tow. Beverly is firmly cemented to her chair and does not dare move the smallest muscle. She really wishes she could just hide under the table.

Marilyn waves to the girls like a celebrity until she sees Beverly, by now starting to sink deep into her booth chair. Marilyn's facial expression changes to very serious (maybe even angry) and she motions for Mary to follow her. Mary immediately obeys and they seem to be arguing in whispers as they head into the lady's restroom.

When Mary returns (without Marilyn), she doesn't sit back down at the table. Instead, she stands behind Beverly with her hands on her shoulders and says to the girls at the table in a cool, matter-of-fact voice, "I hate to break the party up, but Beverly and I need to get going. Our boss is having a party tonight and we need to 'show up' – if you know what I mean . . ." The girls all laugh. "Are you ready, Beverly?"

"Sure." Beverly says with uncertainly. Mary helps her up and leads her toward the dreaded restroom. Beverly stammers, "Are you crazy? Where are we going?"

She imagines that Marilyn is waiting for her there, so she protests with a full sum of fear vibrating in her heart. She plants her feet firmly outside the restroom door and notices that Mary is also shaking.

Mary quickly whispers in a calming tone, "Marilyn wants to know why you are here. I told her we were friends, but she is suspicious. We have to get out of here, OK?"

"So, why are we going to the restroom?"

"Don't be ridiculous! Come on!" She grabs Beverly's arm and practically drags her past the restroom, directly into the kitchen. In the kitchen there is a tall and handsome Hispanic man with a dirty white apron and a fair amount of white hair in his sideburns, contrasting shiny black hair.

"Maria Mary! What's up? You shouldn't be in here, you know," he teases.

"Hi, Juan! I wanted you to meet my friend, Beverly!" Mary says with a big grin on her face.

"¡Hola! Any friend of Maria's is a friend of mine!" He kisses Beverly's hand dramatically.

Mary is obviously in a hurry, "I need a favor, Juan. Could we exit using the back door? I met a real bitch in there and I am afraid she wants a fight."

"I suppose so, but don't make this a habit, OK? I really should not even let you in here! Don't tell anyone I did, OK?" he says, his accent more pronounced as he flusters a bit.

Mary kisses Juan smack on the lips and they head out the back door. "I won't! Adios!"

"Adios Maria!"

Soon the two frightened women are running awkwardly down the alley in high heels. By the time they reach the sidewalk both are out of breath. The walkway is littered with a large assortment of night people and the associated street noise, trash, and busyness, giving them some anonymity for at least a couple minutes.

"Now what?" Beverly asks, puffing, flushed and sweating profusely. She is pulling her dress down, but it still feels ridiculously short.

"Did you bring your camera like I asked?"

"Yes, but what would we be taking pictures of right now? I thought we were going to take pictures of Marilyn with the girls, but I think we missed that opportunity."

"I thought we could wait in a place where we can see Marilyn's motorcycle and get a good picture of her getting on it with her friends."

"Excuse my ignorance, Mary, but what good would THAT do now? I thought we were going to take a picture of the group, and then get Marilyn and Nancy drunk so that they would confess. You were going to record that, remember? Now I am not even sure why we are here."

"When I told Bob about Marilyn, he laughed at me." Mary replies defensively. "I need to prove that she has a second life that he has never seen."

"OK . . . How will that prove that Marilyn murdered Ellen?"

"Maybe we can't prove that today, but we can prove that she is different than what everyone thinks!"

"So, this is two-part plan? Mary, I don't think I could do this again!"

"We may have to improvise. Do you have a better plan?"

"If that is all we are here for tonight, why can't we just look in the bar window and get a picture of her in the bar?"

"OK! Let's try!" Mary responds like a football coach.

Slowly Mary and Beverly venture up to the window where Marilyn just happens to be staring straight at them! Panicked, the flustered women run back into the crowd towards Mary's car.

In reality, Marilyn did not even see them at the window. She is too obsessed with noodling what the heck happened to them, now that she knows that Mary did not bring Beverly to the restroom like she asked. She has sent one of her followers to check around the other tables and look upstairs. When she returns empty handed, Marilyn demands that her biker friends follow her and they congregate on the street.

Marilyn looks at the gaggle of women and says, "I smell trouble, but fortunately, I know where trouble lives!" With that, she leads her group to their bikes and they all take off together with Marilyn in the lead.

* * * * *

Neither Beverly nor Mary can decide where they should go or what they should do. They have been yelling at each other ever since they got in the car and both are shaking uncontrollably as they speed down the downtown streets.

"We should go to the Police!" Beverly insists.

"Why? We don't have any proof of anything and they will just think we are completely nuts. I believe that Marilyn will probably go to my house."

"Why would she go there?"

"Because she knows me and knows that I tipped you off and left with you!"

"Is Ivan at home?"

"No. He's with my mother."

"Well, if that gang goes to my house, I have children there!"

Mary pulls the car over to the curb, turns off the lights and the engine and calmly says, "She won't go to your house, but she will go to my house. She is mad at me because I took you away from the bar when she asked me to arrange for you and her to talk."

"About what?"

"I have no idea, but I suspect she was going to find out what you know about the murders."

"I don't know ANYTHING!"

"You know more than you share, even if you don't believe you do. I am so mad at you right now! We are going to MY house."

"What if you are wrong?"

"I'm not," Mary says decisively and starts her car back up.

"Why would we go where we expect them to be going?"

"We need to get some evidence against Marilyn. We can't get it without a confrontation."

"We could get killed."

"Maybe, but our kids will be safe."

Beverly is so mad and shocked that she cannot respond. Mary speeds a full twenty miles over the speed limit to her house. The driveway is dark, silent and foreboding, but Mary wastes no time in opening the garage door.

Beverly's eyes show intense fear, "What if they are already here, Mary?"

"How could they be? They did not know where we were going and we left first," Mary responds curtly. She checks her purse for her phone and then runs into the house, motioning for Beverly to stay put. When she returns, she grabs an aluminum ladder from the garage and demands, "Follow me."

Beverly has her phone in her hand, but has not decided who to call. She reluctantly follows Mary who uses her phone to close the garage door.

Clumsily, they walk on high-heels through the jagged rocks of the zero-scaped home. "Are you going to call the police?" Beverly asks. "Do you have a plan?"

The dogs next door are now barking loudly. Mary responds to Beverly with an order, "Make sure your phone has the ringer turned off.

161

Damn dogs!" She sets the ladder up against the house. "COME ON! We have to hurry!"

"Where are we going?" Beverly asks, incredulous to Mary's ambition to do what appears to be absolutely insane. Mary throws her heels over the fence at the dogs and then climbs the ladder with the wind immodestly blowing her dress up to reveal the cheeks of her butt in thong underwear. The barking increases.

"Just trust me!" Mary yells down to Beverly. Her face looks haggard for such a young woman and frightened, but she seems totally sure of what she is doing. "Throw your shoes over the fence to the dogs!"

Beverly does not know what to do but trust Mary. She throws her shoes to the dogs, increasing their fervor. As she pauses at the ladder bottom, she hears the back door open next door and someone whistle and then call the dogs. Mary makes the "Shush!" sound with her finger and Beverly freezes in place, her bare feet aching on the bottom rung of the ladder.

The dogs make a few more pointed barks before they run to their owner. "What's the matter with you two?" A male voice asks the dogs. The moments click by as he gives the dogs pats to calm them down and finally takes them into the house with him.

"Come on!" Mary whispers with urgency, peering over the rooftop. Hearing motorcycles up the road, Beverly's heart leaps out of rhythm as she scurries up to the roof, each step with agonizing pain. Once Beverly gets her footing on the roof, Mary picks up the ladder and carefully places it on the neighbor's side of the 6-foot fence, letting it fall with a thud on their grass.

The loud reverberation of several motorcycles entering the driveway terrifies the two women who position themselves flat on their stomachs on the roof. Beverly finds the scratchy graveled roof unforgiving as she scrapes both knees getting to her lay-down position. The engines quiet and the two roof occupants hear a familiar, low woman's voice say, "She's here. I know it!"

Two grown woman tuck their dresses tightly under them and lay as flat as they can, face down on the garage roof on the dark side of the house in silence, numb with fear. Risking not even a slight move for comfort, they can hear each other's shallow breaths.

Beverly cannot see a good outcome from their circumstance. A chilly wind challenges her strength. Clenching her eyes shut, she tries to translate what is happening by distinguishing sounds.

She hears scuffling near the garage door; low voices and whispering that she cannot understand; an owl hooting; locusts; dogs barking down the street somewhere; and the wind rustling through the trees. Soon she hears voices and footsteps in the backyard. Pulling deeper inside herself, she can hear the blood pumping in her ears. It is not just the scraping of the roof tiles that burns, but also the hurt in her throat and the tears in her eyes. She prays like she has never prayed before. 'Please God, let me live to see my children again. Watch over Mary and me. Jesus, I trust in you." Finishing her prayer, she can feel the warmth of Mary lying next to her, silent as a dead woman.

There is the sound of the front door opening and then closing, low voices and whispering, and then all goes silent for several seconds as they realize some of the women are in the house. The next sound engulfs Beverly and Mary into terror. The garage door opens with a din that vibrates the roof violently where two women cling like barnacles.

"Mary! We know you are here!" a woman's voice tempts loudly and the other woman pipe in, "We see your car!"

"She's here."

"She may have gone to a neighbor's," someone offers.

The garage door closes again jarring the two women on top again. For a few seconds, only footsteps and the women in the backyard can be heard, but it is soon clear that all of the women are now in the backyard as they begin to speak out loud. It seems like forever to Beverly and Mary who wait in silence as the wind blows away any warmth and a slow drizzle of rain assaults their stiff bodies.

Beverly wonders how the heck she got herself into this mess. Could Mary be praying, too? Does God fall for dumb blondes? To appease herself, she muses that for once, Mary's naïve, cutesy vivacious blonde attitude is not going to save her, but her thoughts are interrupted with the sound of cars racing down the driveway.

"Someone's coming!" someone says loudly in the back yard, right before Beverly and Mary hear the distinct sound of frightened whispers and footsteps thudding through the rocks on the side of the house near the garage. The only words Beverly can make out for sure are obscenities.

A car door opens and several sets of footsteps run towards the fleeing women saying, "Stop where you are! This is the Police."

Beverly feels Mary struggling up to see what is happening, but does not feel any compulsion to move. She clings to the roof with her eyes closed, listening to the scuffle below.

Recognizing police voices recanting the Miranda rights, Beverly finally forces herself to open her eyes and in the darkness she sees the scattering light of police cars in the yard. Mary is sitting up next to her.

"Help! We are up here!" Mary calls out loudly with her pathetic high voice.

"How did they know to come?" Beverly asks incredulously, finally coming to her senses.

"I told you I had a plan," replied Mary. "I called 911 on the land line in the house before I came out and hid the phone under my bed. The police always investigate when someone calls 911 and leave the line open. Ivan did it accidentally once and really got me in trouble. Did you know they can charge people for false 911 calls?"

The rest of the night is a blur for Beverly with all the questioning and waiting for paperwork to be filled out. She did find time to ask Mary a question that had burned in her for a very long time. "Mary, why were you monitoring the hallways as *Gerry's Socks & Shoes?*"

"Why would you think I did that? I have always suspected Nancy did it, because she was very interested in the set-up at my daycare where I can watch Ivan from work."

"You saved my life, Mary."

"No. We saved each other. We both needed to know what Marilyn has been hiding."

"But do we know that? As far as I can see, all we have is that they scared us to death and trespassed."

"I think we have more than that."

"Like what?"

"I did not set up a monitor in the hallways at work, but I did set one up at home. I bet that Marilyn or someone from her gang at least said something stupid to incriminate them."

164

"I hope you are right. If not, we looking pretty ridiculous – and could be in more danger than before."

After hours of questioning, Beverly returns home just a little before three o'clock in the morning and finds her house quiet. She is relieved that the kids are sleeping, because she would REALLY have a tough time explaining her outfit, tousled hair and drooping makeup. Surprisingly, she drifts off to sleep almost as soon as her head touches the pillow.

Chapter 30: Blunders

With comprehensive reports filled out and filed, Detectives Simmons and Dell are exhausted as they share a quiet moment over coffee in the department break room. Simmons surmises, "Well, I believe we caught the bad guys."

"Yes, but chances are that it will take some really good lawyers to piece it all together."

"It's too bad that with all the conversation going on, all that could be captured on that open 911 call was Marilyn giving orders to kill Mary and Beverly."

"Well, two women close to the defendants related that the defendants bragged about the killings when they were drunk. We also found the poison used to kill Anna in Nancy's house, but I think she was acting on Marilyn's orders. It will be a shame if Nancy has to take the brunt of the conviction if Marilyn was the boss."

"Well, most people would not carry out orders to kill someone. She deserves to be punished if she did it! You know it would have been an open-and-shut case if those two idiots on the roof had been killed!" Dell teases.

Simmons' laughs, "No, it is just unfortunate that from here on out the whole case will rest on the small amount of evidence we have, testimonies tainted with loyalties, misinterpretations of the truth, and hearsay."

"Isn't that the way it always is? I think that breaking and entering and threatening to kill will get Marilyn some time – and who knows? There could be enough evidence collected in the next few days to put her away."

"It seems the motives for the murders stemmed from some twists of love and jealously that go beyond outrageous. Some people just are so darn stupid."

"Well . . . and let's not forget greedy. Those rings were pretty expensive!" Dell chuckles, "I keep thinking about those women clinging to the roof! Who was that one woman? Beverly? She just INSISTED on being a detective and got herself in more trouble than she ever bargained for!"

"Ah yes, Beverly," Simmons grins. "Her statement said that she found the gun in Anna's desk on the day Anna died. She should have reported that one!"

"For sure! It's difficult to piece the story together. One of the women told me that she heard Nancy brag that she had poisoned Anna's soft drink, which matches what the coroner found as the reason for her death. But, how did she get the body in the restroom?"

"Anna must have gone to the restroom when she began to feel sick," Simmons studies her pencil. "What threw me off was Nancy's fabricated testimony that Mary planned Ellen's murder."

"It appears that she also told that story to Cindy. I think Nancy and Marilyn used gossip to throw us off track."

Dell breaks out in full laughter, "All I can say is what in the world were those two women thinking when they decided to hide on a roof? Did you see the skinned knees? Oh my gosh!"

Both detectives start a laughing fit that neither can shake.

When Simmons gets a little composure, she adds, "Reminds me of that case where that gal decided to set up a swing under a bridge to get a picture of her husband with another woman! It took a mountain rescue team to get her off the high swing!"

"How about the case where the crook robbed a convenience store, wrapped the money up like a present, and then asked his mother to refrain from opening the present until her birthday ten months away? Not much for surprises, she opened it and (surprise!) found over two-thousand dollars in cash! She called the police, realizing that her penniless adult son who was living in her home for free and eating her food must have been the guy who robbed the local convenience store."

Perhaps it is just because they are so tired, but both detectives become giddy as they reminisce, bantering back and forth about some of the dumbest crooks and "hobbyist" detectives they have ever met.

Chapter 31: Midlife Fairytales

Mary is sitting on Ivan's bed, watching him play with his remote control when there is a knock at the door. Reluctantly, she goes to answer it, carefully checking the peek hole before opening the door. Through the small lens she sees someone she is not expecting and opens the door.

Like a guilty dog, she stands looking at him with her large blue eyes tearing up.

"I'm glad you took a couple days off. From the gossip, it sounds like you have been through an awful lot," Bob starts.

Mary looks down at her shoes, "Yes."

"I have something for you, if you still want it."

Mary looks up and sees what Bob is holding and cannot believe her eyes. In his hands he holds her engagement ring. "But, we broke up – does this mean that you still want to marry me?"

"Yes. I have been thinking about it for a long time. I think that Ellen's death made me feel guilty about our affair and rightfully so. It complicated our relationship and made it difficult for me to treat you the way I wanted to." His tears begin to fall and chin quivers. "We were both wrong in having an affair, but God forgives and we need to forgive each other. I believe . . . that we belong together, through thick and thin, until death do we part."

"Wow – Really?" Mary oozes in her high-pitched voice.

"Would it be too much to ask that we go to counseling and try to piece what we have back together? I would also like to start going to a church that I went to years ago."

"I would like to get back into my church, but any church would be better than none. I just feel I need to start looking more closely at the life I am living. I want to be a good person."

"You are a good person, Mary. So – counseling and church? Think we can bring our little families together and work towards a better life for all of us?"

"Yes. That's what I want!" Mary falls into his arms.

After a good hug and kiss, Bob gets down on one knee and puts the ring on Mary's finger. He then looks up to see Ivan standing shyly by his bedroom door. "Come on, Ivan! Let's go celebrate! Where do you want to eat?"

"McDonalds."

Bob and Mary look at each other, Bob shrugs, and they head off to a restaurant they never would have picked to celebrate with Ivan.

* * * * *

Beverly and Bill sit on the couch in Beverly's living room. "So you thought that hiding all the dangerous and difficult things going on was better for me and the kids?" Bill asks, obviously amazed and angry at the choices she has made.

Beverly is in tears, "No one would have believed what was going on. You have no idea how hard this was for me! I couldn't tell anyone about our plan, because I wasn't sure if it would work and everyone already believed I was crazy!"

Bill sighs with disgust and looks away. "No one said you were crazy." Silence paces between them, holding feelings hostage. Finally in resignation, he rises from the sofa and starts for the door.

Tania races out of her room sobbing, "Don't leave, Bill! Mom, why are you letting him leave?"

Beverly is now sobbing.

Bill looks at Tania soberly and says, "Tania, I really do love you, your mom and the boys, but people need to be able to share what's going on in their life. I just can't stop thinking of the danger your mother was in and how she did not reach out to me for help."

"Would you have believed her if she told you what was going on and would you have stood behind her if you knew her plan?" Tania demands.

Bill wipes away evidence of tears. Both of Beverly's boys show up and stand behind Tania. No one knows what to say or do. Bill slowly walks back to sit next to Beverly on the couch. Her children stand nearby, unable to express their feelings.

"You know," Jason says, "she's been very brave."

Bill can only nod, but his eyes do meet Beverly's.

Beverly pulls herself together and looks up at Bill to say, "There are some things that you have to go through alone. I could not share this with you! I had only suspicions, not any concrete evidence, and a gut feeling. I am lucky that Mary and I were not killed and I know that."

"I only understand that you put yourself in danger and I never want for that to happen again."

"I can't promise nothing bad will ever happen or that we will all live happily ever after."

"I know, but from now on, if we are going to be friends, we need to share what is going on in our lives, ok?"

Beverly's tear-stained eyes meet his. "I want to share everything with you, but this time it was all too bazaar and confusing and I did not want you to see me as a drama queen."

"I'm sorry," Bill answers slyly, "but you definitely fit in the 'drama queen' shoes this time."

Life seems suspended for a couple minutes as Beverly and Bill remain silent and the kids fidget on the sidelines waiting for some sign that all can be forgiven.

"Someday, you know, we will probably laugh about this," Beverly finally says.

"I don't think so," Bill says wryly.

"Well, probably not for a long while, but the details are so ridiculous that I just don't see how we would not laugh someday." Beverly's mouth pulls into a shy smile as she continues, "It may be funnier than you think, Bill! Well, I know murder and capital crimes are never funny, but sometimes the circumstances you get into trying to figure it all out are pretty funny."

"It will be a long time before I can laugh at this."

"I do wish we could have pinned those women with all the crimes Mary and I believe they committed, but I guess I've figured out by now that life is just not that perfect. At least we got them for something!"

Bill puts his arm around her and a chill of relief trickles down Beverly's spine. "You know," she continues, "another thing I have been hiding from you is that I am writing a novel."

"Really? Well, I did not know you were a writer. Are you writing about this?"

"No, my book is fiction. God knows that life is hard enough without trying to explain to friends and relatives why you painted them the way you did in a book!"

"I imagine that is true. I would really like to read your book when it is finished." Beverly and Bill move closer together. "What other secrets do you hold?" His face holds the promise of a smile.

"I guess we will need to work on learning each other's secrets." Beverly responds.

"I'm hoping you don't have too many more!"

Jason motions for Tania and Mark to leave the room. Tania is reluctant, but Jason narrows his eyes to let her know who's boss.

* * * * *

That night after Bill has taken his leave, Beverly ready's herself for bed, choosing her favorite pink cotton night shirt. Turning out the light, she pulls the familiar soft covers up to her chin. As she stares up at the ceiling, she remembers her dark writings about a young battered heroine who suffered things no young girl should have to suffer and saved her world without even an inkling of what she was doing or how it would affect her village. All she was trying to do was sort out what had happened to her and what she could do to stop the evil that she could not understand.

What distinguishes right and wrong when the world seems turned completely up-side-down? Surely the Ten Commandments cover most anything someone could do wrong under normal circumstances, but do circumstances change or at least alter the rules?

As Beverly examines this, she remembers verses from the Bible that she rarely thinks about and does not have memorized. Reaching to the table beside her bed for her Bible, she finds the verses she is searching for in Ecclesiastes:

To everything there is a season and a time to every purpose under the heaven: a time to be born, and a time to die; a time to plant, and a time to pluck up that which is planted . . .

From the depth of her soul, Beverly thanks God that the ending of this portion of her life-story turned out abundantly better than the fate of the young heroin in her story. She relishes that she has another day to contemplate life and enjoy those who love her. Sleep tantalizes her senses as she gives thanks for all those who sing the slow, sweet harmony of freedom, goodwill and appreciation while aspiring to live fruitfully and generously in a world full of jealousy and greed.

Beverly's fairy tales of how life should be have disintegrated. Bill is more than she deserves and from now on, she will work very hard on their relationship. She has had him on the back burner, but now she knows that he is exactly the person she hopes will share the rest of her life.

Villains are not always foiled, but most do eventually fall. There may not be enough evidence to convict Marilyn and Nancy of both murders. In fact, there is a slight possibility that they may only be charged with trespassing and verbal assault, but Detective Simmons seemed confident that there will be enough evidence to convict both women for at least one of the murders. Beverly is confident that the detectives, lawyers and all others who are trained to work with crime will do the best they can to get the bad guys.

Before drifting completely off into dreamland, Beverly praises God for Mary, her hero, who is not as dumb or self-centered as she paints herself. Mary thought on her feet that night as they shivered in the cold together. She was able to formulate a plan at a time when Beverly was frozen with fear and completely out of ideas.

To Beverly, Mary will always be an odd friend, difficult to understand, quite self-indulged; but always sweet, beautiful and treasured by men who cannot resist her cleavage; and irritating to women who do not understand her personality. Hopefully, she has learned something about the type of friends she keeps, but probably not. Mary will always be fragile, but agile and free as a butterfly, flitting through life without ever realizing that much of the drama in her life is the consequence of the choices she makes.

'Well, at least life with Mary is never boring!' Beverly surmises. And then she starts to giggle uncontrollably as a picture emerges in her mind of two silly women throwing their shoes to the dogs, climbing up to the roof in flamboyant dresses, and lying flat on the rooftop like idiots waiting for their fate. After a good laugh at herself, sleep comes blissfully with a feeling of well-being that she has not had for a very long time.

Coming Soon

Family Untied, Lives Entwined
Corky Reed-Watt

A child is stolen from her bed and nineteen years later, three mothers' lives have continued on and a young girl has grown up. One of the mothers is her broken-hearted biological mother. Another mother helped with a fraudulent adoption and the third adopted the child.

When the truth becomes clear, an ethical decision must be made that will affect the futures of many people, including the young woman, the mothers, and the extended families. Who will make that decision and what will it be?

About the Author

Corky Reed-Watt has written local magazine articles, training materials, and even speeches, but this is her first attempt at a novel. She is the mother of five, a grandmother, and a great-grandmother. Her hobbies include painting, glass fusing, needlework, gardening and sewing. During the work day she works as a program/project manager for a Fortune 500 technology company, but in her evenings and on weekends, she is Grandma, a writer and an artist.